The Beadworkers

The Beadworkers

Stories

BETH PIATOTE

COUNTERPOINT
Berkeley, California

The Beadworkers

"Feast (Triptych)" was first published in *The Kenyon Review Online*, Jan/Feb
2019. "The News of the Day" was first published in *Studies in American Indian
Literatures* 21.2 (2009). "Beading Lesson" was first published in *Reckonings:
Contemporary Short Fiction by Native American Women*, ed. Hertha D. Sweet Wong,
Lauren Stuart Muller, and Jana Sequoya Magdaleno (Oxford University
Press, 2008).

Library of Congress Cataloging-in-Publication Data
Names: Piatote, Beth H., 1966– author.
Title: The beadworkers / Beth Piatote.
Description: First hardcover edition. | Berkeley, California : Counterpoint,
    2019.
Identifiers: LCCN 2019017873 | ISBN 9781640092686
Subjects: LCSH: Indians of North America—Fiction. | Indians of North
    America—Social life and customs—Fiction. | Northwest, Pacific—Fiction.
Classification: LCC PS3616.I21255 .A6 2019 | DDC 813/.6—dc23
LC record available at https://lccn.loc.gov/2019017873

Jacket design by Jenny Carrow
Book design by Jordan Koluch

COUNTERPOINT
2560 Ninth Street, Suite 318
Berkeley, CA 94710
www.counterpointpress.com

Printed in the United States of America
Distributed by Publishers Group West

10 9 8 7 6 5 4 3 2 1

In honor of my mother, Anne Eagle Hege
In memory of my father, Carl Henry Hege

Contents

wé·tes waẋ waq̓í·swit

land and life

Feast I

kú·s
first taste of life
not air but water, carried
by our mothers, we taste water
rising from earth, turning in salt waters where
you **nasóʔx̣** travel
through ocean waves and
darkness gaining power
in those far away salt
currents of sea and labor
to return again
to the cold river of your origin
upriver to give life
where **wewúkiye** bugle
in fog-mantled mornings of our
land awakening we step
toward **ʔímes** each foot
fall a quiet petition to be worthy of your
gift, we bring you in, carry you
adorned in beadwork and beauty
as drums beat
through heart and women sing

łitá·n

songs return to
earth, belong
to the land, gathered by
hand thick bitter taste of
green hills **qémes** cradled
in your hand, rooting
you to this place, songs
flow from our throats a
fine rain, the water cycle
gives **qá·ws** in spring
first feast of our green
returning
sun grows long branches
reach to sky, hungry birds
share **tíms** offering
hard seeds to roll on our tongues
with succulent sound of our
ni·mi·pu·tímt
we sing **cemí·tx** mountains
in new dresses with baskets woven
by grandmothers' hands and songs
we carry, we are carried
to return again, give thanks again, return these songs
give breath and good words, ring, lift hands
to sky release heart thoughts, we
are borne in
kú·s

Feast II

kú·s

I had a dream not long after I started. Some people say that when you start dreaming in a language, that is when you know it has become fluent to you, but I know this can't possibly be so. I think I maybe knew twenty or thirty words at the time, mostly nouns and greetings and a few verbs. But I had this dream, and it was beautiful. In the dream I saw the longhouse at Nespelem, and on the side of the longhouse I saw clearly this word: PÁ·YN. *Arrival.* I woke just then, suddenly, and as I woke I heard my own voice say: *pá·yca. I am coming, I am arriving.* The shock of hearing my voice impressed upon me the feeling of the dream. That dream helped me persevere when I felt small, when I was alone, when I looked at the enormity of it all. There were times I was discouraged, when I faced the entire ocean of words and I feared the undertow would pull me under, like an eagle who is dragged into the current of a river, talons locked on the back of a salmon. Later I would learn another word, and I would hold it just as close, say it to myself, to the sky, say it to Phil and those who spoke: *pá·yca pá·ytoqsa.* I am coming. *I am coming back.*

nasóʔx̱

He was from a Salmon Tribe over that way, over to the coast.
And his tribe got terminated.
I don't know why, but the folks around there stopped. Maybe
it was a dark time for them. But they gave up the Salmon Cere-
mony, all them. Except this *one guy*.
That's not something to do with just one person, but he did.
Not even his family came. Some of his own people got on him.
Went hard on him for doin' that. And maybe it wasn't right, to do
it that way, just he alone. I know that man. He's stubborn! He don't
care. Eight, maybe ten years like that, he kept it up, all alone.
After that people started coming back.
Now you go over there to Salmon Ceremony with them, and
there's hundreds of people there. Not even all them know this
story, but it's true.

wewúkiye

The animals help us. We know this from the old stories from when
the world was coming to be, and the animal people offered them-
selves to us, each in their way, each one in order. And still they
offer themselves to us. A few years ago, I saw a photograph in
the newspaper of a ship in the Pacific Ocean, headed north. The
ship was bearing the ancestors and belongings of the Haida Gwaii
people. The ship was carrying them back home, bringing them
home from a museum. So there was the ship, headed north. And
in front of the ship, leading the procession, was a bald eagle flying
in the sky. And swimming alongside the ship, cresting with the
waves, was a pod of killer whales. They traveled that way all along
the Pacific Coast, all the way home.

The animals help us. We know this from the old stories, from family stories, from court stories. I know a story that is happening right now, about a man who called on an elk to help him, and the elk came to his aid, and now the man is in court. But listen. This is a good story. You see, the man is Sinixt from north of here. Many years ago, the Sinixt people were suffering from smallpox. They were weakened, and the Canadian miners and settlers hunted those people down, drove them out of their homeland. The survivors came to us for refuge. We took them in, and now they are strong again. Here we call them the Lakes people. But they never stopped wanting to go back, or going back, in fact, to visit their homelands and hunt. Canada, in the meantime, decided the Sinixt were extinct and extinguished their rights. But the Sinixt people are still alive and so are their rights.

A few years ago one of these unextinct Sinixt men killed an elk in his homelands. Then he called the game officials in Canada and turned himself in. They took the bait. When the province pressed charges against him for taking big game without a license, he pleaded not guilty. He cited his aboriginal rights to hunt in his own territory. And now that case is in court, and Canada will have to look at that man, standing in the middle of the room, and all his people around him, and Canada will have to admit that the Sinixt are not extinct. The Sinixt man is very brave. And so is the elk who gave himself. That man and that elk knew each other from long ago; they met in dreams and sweat, blood and forest. The man needed the elk; the people need the elk. Without the elk, there would be no case, no path home, no court for the man to present himself to the State and say: *we are alive.*

ʔímes

From the Colville Confederated Tribes TANF (Temporary Assistance for Needy Families) Survey:

- What are the responsibilities of a father?
- What are the responsibilities of an uncle?
- Should a deer be considered acceptable payment in lieu of cash?

łitá·n

And this one, you need to remember this. This root is good for nursing mothers.

qémes

After World War II, advances in astrophysics allowed humans to see their planet from space. In 1972, the Apollo 17 took the most famous photograph of Earth, the blue planet. It might be fair to say that since the mid-twentieth century, humans have seen things that were never within their visual grasp before. But do we have better dreams? Have we seen better things? I think I would give up my fridge magnet of Planet Earth, every glimpse of snowy mountain folds from the window of a plane, the glittering view of Paris from the Eiffel Tower on New Year's Eve—I would give up all of these things to see what our ancestors saw, to dream their vivid dreams, to come over a mountain with my mothers and sisters and suddenly see, in the wide open, an enormous blue meadow of blooming camas, an endless, unbroken field of periwinkle, lake, and lapis that today you could barely imagine, a land breathing and rolling with blue, a land so beautiful that you would wonder how to find your voice, find your offering, draw out

a song on your breath and press the strength of your body to the earth, into the earth, into the deep wild blue.

qáˑws

From the Treaty of 1855:

Article III

The exclusive right of taking fish in all the streams where running through or bordering said reservation is further secured to said Indians: as also the right of taking fish at all usual and accustomed places in common with citizens of the territory, and of erecting temporary buildings for curing, together with the privilege of hunting, gathering roots and berries, and pasturing their horses and cattle upon open and unclaimed land.

tíms

We had been camping for several days, and then we packed up to go home. It was August. Hot. And we were going down a dry, dusty mountain road when we saw these big bushes loaded with chokecherries, right beside a little stream. We stopped there and picked until we filled two big buckets, which took a long time, and I have to admit we were not the most agreeable children at that time. We were tired and sweaty and wanted to go home. But my parents simply could not drive past those trees aflame with ripeness. We picked, we complained, we spit out the bright red ones—too bitter to eat raw, but filled with pectin and good to keep. Our parents did not scold us. The next day my mother and I cooked the fruit down, strained it through cheesecloth, and made jelly. We poured the jelly into a mismatched collection of jars and small glasses, and sealed them with paraffin wax. We laughed at

how long it took to pick those buckets and how much fruit it took
to make each little jar, which, when held to the light of the late-
afternoon sun, cast a rosy glow on the kitchen table.

cemí·tx

. . . ʔiceyé·ye hiʔsé·pte kamó·twalc pá·x̣at, ka· papćícqi ka· ʔáps
ʔá·likaʔs. capáypa ćixćíxne luk̓úpluk̓úp pé·kuya ka hé·nek̓e
pá·tyoxna, "ʔilcwé····ẃcix! kíye pí·wetemeyleksix." koní·x wáqoʔ
pé·tqexne ćíxćix hilk̓ú·pluk̓u·pce ka hihíne, "wéye ʔi·m nisé·ẃeylu,
kawó' ʔí·nanɋo'c mú·xsnim, wetemeylékim." wáqo' ka· ʔiceyé·yenm
péhinewye ka· ʔinekí·k̓u' ɋo' tiwíwtiwíw ʔilcwe·ẃcix hikó·qana.
koná ʔiceyé·yenm pé·ne, "kawó' ʔí·ne weteméylekim—wáqo'
ʔóykalana titó·qana ʔekú·s ʔé·. kawó' ʔí·nenk̓u', ké·n····ex tillá·pno'."
kuʔús peɋsisimnúye. ka· wáqo' pétemeyleke ʔilcwé·ẃcisnim. kála
konmá pé·ʔnehneme ʔiceyé·yene koná páʔnixqawna titlúqawsna
ka· titlúcemitexne ka· titlúkikeyene, "kíne titó·qanm pá·ʔya·x̣cano'
ka· hipalló·yno'. kí·mtemcimk̓eẏ hiwéhyem netí·telwit." . . .

. . . Coyote carried on his back five agate knives and pure
fir pitch and flint for making a fire. After some time, he made
the grasses sway and again Coyote shouted to the monster,
"ʔilcwéeeeẃcix! Let's inhale each other!" At that point, Monster
suddenly saw the grasses moving and he said, "Now, then, you
little Nisé·ẃeylu, you first inhale me!" Then Coyote tried, and he
made Monster stagger a little bit. Coyote said to him, "Now me
you inhale—now that everyone, all the titó·qana you have just
eaten. Take me, too, lesssssst I become lonely." Thus he insisted.
And now the monster inhaled him. Just that way Monster took
Coyote in, and as he went flying through the air, Coyote placed
each one along the way, the titlú-roots and titlú-huckleberries
and titlú-service berries, saying: *Here the Indian People will find them,*

and they will be happy. In only a short time away, the human beings are coming . . .

Rain came in abundance after years of drought in California, and we had no desire to complain about the gift of water. We wore our boots and beaded medicine bags and assembled on the steps, held our soggy banners aloft. Some of us had been to the camp, some not. We each did what we could. I marched with thousands in DC, also in the rain, and later sent money and supplies. I followed the stories of tribal delegations and ordinary activists to Oceti Sakowin, protests in Spokane, Seattle, the Capitol. We shouted, we marched, we wrote, we prayed, we drummed and sang and rang bells. We lifted our hands with eagle feathers and banners and holy anger, the anger of Jesus storming the temple, the holy fire of Chief Joseph, Sitting Bull, Martin Luther King. I saw my kin lean against the bitter winter with hand-lettered signs that said KÚ·S HÍ·WES WÁ·Q̓IS. *Water is life. Water is alive.* All life begins and ends with water: our mothers, the rivers, the rain. From the beginning of time to the end of time, the word we carry on our breath, the taste of this world on our tongues and our tears, is alive, is life, is **kú·s**

Feast III

Water coughed from the mouth of the hand pump, smacking the floor of the metal bucket, which tipped suddenly from the force. With one hand, Mae reached to steady the pail, whose handle was looped on the neck of the pump, and with the other she pushed the arm of the pump to weaken its stream. The water flowed smoothly then, filling the bucket quickly, and Mae cranked down again to stop it. Mae knew that the water would be frigid, but nonetheless she dipped her hand, cupped, to break its surface, and slurped the drawn coldness from her palm. Emptied, her hand retained the shock of iciness, feeling to her like another substance, not at all her own body, but weighty, slick, and cold as the underside of a salmon just pulled from the river.

She wiped her hand quickly on her dungarees and unhitched the pail, then filled a second one. It was easier to carry two than one, and less likely to spill. She anchored herself and lifted both buckets, striding evenly toward the camp. As she walked, she took in the sounds: the low rumble of mourning doves in the barn, a blackbird's hail, the swish of grass against her leg. Without warning she flashed upon a memory of herself as a child, losing control of a washbucket and mop in the hallway of the girls' dormitory at Carlisle. Miss Lunsford had barked angrily at her, accusing Mae of carelessness and *sloth*, and the sudden fury had

caused such tension, as Mae and all the girls froze in place, that Mae was overcome with the impulse to laugh. She had fought hard against it as the urge tugged at the corners of her mouth. She tried to breathe evenly and stare at the floor, but the pressure was too much. Just as the water had liberated itself from the washbucket, the laugh escaped her mouth. The girls stared, wide-eyed, as Miss Lunsford seized Mae by the arm and dragged her to the supply closet, shutting her in the dark with only her thoughts and the stinging smell of lye to surround her. Her eyes and lungs burned. None of the other girls had laughed. But later, retelling the story outside under a tree, with Mae their returned hero and Miss Lunsford's reaction on vivid replay, they laughed until their stomachs ached. Mae smiled then, remembering her school chums.

She set the buckets down beside the stove and used a dipper to fill the enamel coffee pot and toss in some grounds. The stove was the central fixture of the camp kitchen, which was really no more than a stove and a table on a platform under a pitched roof. The kitchen and the outhouse were the only structures with any permanence in the camp. At the worktable, Annie was cutting flour with lard for biscuits. Mae could hear others in the camp stirring. Faintly she heard a man singing "When You're Smiling," the sound muffled by a canvas tipi wall. Its source was the far side of the encampment, near the farmer's house. She remembered Jim getting dressed in the morning and singing to himself, then pushed the image out of her mind. She missed his voice. His hands. His gentle nature. Mornings were always the worst; grief like fog only lifted as the day wore on. Still, these mornings had been a bit easier. While for some of them, the labor camp was a departure from life's ordinary comforts—a wooden door, a soft chair, a reliable icebox—for Mae it was a welcome escape from

the thunderous stillness of the small, stick-built house that she had once shared with Jim and their daughter, Jeannette.

Annie glanced up from her bowl and asked Mae to look after the beans. The pot was heavy; Mae lifted it gingerly and clamped the lid slightly askew with her thumbs, lugging it to the edge of the platform and tipping the pot to drain off the soaking water. This took time and finesse, but she managed it, then delivered the pot to the stove top, covering the beans in fresh water. The pot would dutifully simmer all day, while the crew was in the orchard.

"Mae, I had a dream last night," Annie said. "I was picking cherries."

They laughed. It was always the case that two or three days into the harvest, everyone would be dreaming about picking cherries—or strawberries, plums, peaches, hops, or apples— whatever crop demanded their attention. Sometimes these dreams would morph into gigantesque wildness—trees multiplying across an endless plain, or fruit appearing the size of lambs, or canvas drop cloths knee-deep with the ruby flesh of plums. When the chiefs were summoned to this valley in 1855 for treaty talks, the Americans said this: *you will walk in blood knee-deep if you do not sign.* Now the valley was bursting with orchards, and the Indians begged the agents for passes to follow the harvests all summer. They were migrant workers in their own land, a fact they accepted by day but questioned in their sleep.

"I'd like to count those bushels I picked all night," Annie said.

"Once I dreamt I had to eat everythin' I picked," Mae said. "Worse than the pickin' dream."

"Ooh, I get that one, too," Annie replied. "All summer, same dreams."

Mae hadn't eaten a single cherry or other piece of fresh fruit for nearly a year, either in waking or in dream life. After a death, a

person ate only dried food for a set of seasons, until the memorial. Jim died in September, after Jeannette had gone back to Chemawa. Mae's friends brought her offerings of smoked salmon and dried venison all winter. She tasted every recipe on the reservation. Now, in late spring, new cherries dripped from lush branches. She contemplated a small bucket of fruit that had been set aside for eating—the farmer always let them have whatever they could eat. She tried to conjure desire for the sweet, juicy taste. But she felt nothing. Perhaps some part of her had died. Perhaps it was just the natural antipathy of the day harvester for the harvest.

She could see that everyone was up by now and headed to the stove. Everyone would take coffee, and most would eat food they brought from home. The farmer's wife had left them a large glass jar filled with milk for the children, though they didn't care so much for the grassy taste, and sometimes complained of stomachaches after. In the schools, they learned to drink weak coffee, and this was now the universal drink.

There was no leisure to the morning routine, save what one could steal by singing or joking in the course of work. Mae tied her hair, still too short for braids, in a bun at the nape of her neck and popped on her hat. On the first days, she had tied it back in two low ponytails, like a girl. She had surprised herself when she looked in the mirror. A girl! So far was she from the world of floursack skirts and long stockings. Her hands were already chapped and rough from the work, dirt ground into her nails and pads of her fingers. She could feel the sandpapery texture when she rubbed her fingers together.

Still, there was every morning an optimistic sky.

She did not want to admit that there was anything good about her new life, stark as it was. But she did feel something like relief that without Jim she felt less judgmental—or perhaps simply less

aware—of her own hard edges. Next to him, she felt that she was always overwhelming him a bit with her opinions, her loudness, her physicality. Not that he ever said so. No, he would never say so! He was quiet, and when confronted with things he did not like he was absolutely silent. He had that way about him. His death was the greatest silence, of course.

No one knew how it happened. One night he didn't come home from town, where he had been playing the fiddle at a dance, and early the next morning they had found him. Mae felt that this great mystery around his death had attached to her. She could feel it sometimes in the way the others regarded her, as though she were moving about the world with the word HOW? blazed across her chest. Some days she wished she could be like Hester Prynne, except instead of an *A* she would wear a scarlet question mark. She imagined herself beading an elaborate ? in a contoured floral pattern, with a sky-blue background, and affixing it directly to her dresses. She and her friends at school had loved Hester Prynne, the most Indian heroine a white man ever invented. They believed that when Hester disappeared at the end of the book, she had gone to live with the Indians who were always present, watching from the edge of the forest. The Puritan town fathers, the girls thought, reminded them of the Agents back at home.

Not knowing the *how* of Jim's death deferred Mae's query as to *why*. Why would he be taken from this world so suddenly? Why should she be left all alone? It was true that Jim had a weakness for drink, but why should that define his final moments, his life? It was only his gentle nature, his sensitivity, that made him weak. The pain of the world seeped into him, and he had tried to wash it out with work, with drink, with music. He had been tall and lanky, and had dressed in western shirts and straight-leg denims to play

fiddle on Saturday nights in town. He would wear a white straw Stetson and a pair of elaborately beaded floral cuffs—red tulip motif, green leaves, and white background, with copious fringe—on his wrists. He was quiet, but he could dress loud! Mae used to call him Jackson Sundown. When he was on stage, sometimes she would feel the sorrow of his bow pulling across the strings—but he would quickly turn from it, the bow suddenly skipping like a child, the fringe of his cuffs animate with dance. When he played, none of them could stay in their seats—his reels and jigs brought them out. This year would be the first time that the labor camp would be without his playing on Sunday nights. Getting through the first time of everything without him—the first Christmas, the first birthday, the first feast—was the sum purpose of this year. The last feast would arrive in late summer, and soon after would be the anniversary of his death. Just one day, Mae would tell herself, although she knew it wasn't true. A sudden loss like that colored all the days around it, rendering the days before and after into bright, stinging hues, until the event of his death spread over many days, a season unto itself.

In the immediate shock of Jim's passing, Annie and the other ladies had brought Mae willow tea for the pain. Ah, this had been soothing. Later, once the *why* questions set in, they brought her small dry cakes made of ground roots. She received these not with pleasure but with equanimity, with bland recognition that he was gone and she was still here.

A crow cawed loudly from a tree just then. Annie's husband, Frank, was yelling, too, telling them to load up in the truck to get to the fields. Mae noticed something odd then. A blue Ford truck loaded with workers—with men, all men—passed by them on the highway. Frank and some of their men waved. And some of the braceros waved back. Mae watched the truck disappear

Indian Wars

The News of the Day

The mirror fell off the wall, and Marcel knew that his father was dead in another country. Marcel reached his hand to his breast pocket and withdrew his watch from its place near his still-beating heart. The face told him the time, and the minute hand obediently ticked forward. Marcel sat down. He looked at the watch again. He thought of his sister laying the plates on the table for the evening meal. He thought of his mother, face tilted toward the sky, lifting her hand to suspend a crystal snowflake in the window of his father's shop in Paris.

Marcel sat there, staring at the wall that had so recently released the mirror, at the faint outline where sunlight had faded the surface.

Marcel heard the handle of the door click open. Charles entered the room, his books and a newspaper tucked neatly in his arm, pressed snugly against his black overcoat. His shoulders bore the evidence of snowfall, but the flakes were quickly disappearing into the darkness of the wool. His eyes took in the surroundings: the unmade bed, the mirror sprawled on the floor with a jagged crack across its face, Marcel's troubled expression. Charles closed the door quietly behind him. Charles crossed the room to his desk, slipped into his chair, and unfolded his newspaper. He sat, straight-backed, and opened the pages, the grayish newsprint like

a sagging flag in his slender brown fingers. From behind the paper, Charles did not observe Marcel, although it would have been easy enough to do so. Charles was a man who respected another man's dignity.

Marcel continued to stare at the wall.

Charles shifted in his chair.

Snow floated silently from the sky in the fields beyond their shuttered window.

There had been no good news for months. Every day Charles would fortify himself to open the paper, scanning it quickly for dispatches from the correspondents at the Agency. It had been less than two weeks ago that Sitting Bull had died at the hands of Indian police. Sometimes, when he could voice the words, Charles read the news out loud to Marcel, who listened attentively. It was one of the many things Charles appreciated about his friend; Marcel did not resist hearing stories of the military campaigns on Indian lands. Marcel did not flinch at stories of starvation at the Agency or the persistence of the Ghost Dance; he neither defended nor decried the Seventh Cavalry. Marcel could take it in with perfect equanimity—the gift of his foreign blood. Why this was such a blessing Charles could not precisely express.

Occasionally the two men spoke to one another in French, a convergence they discovered soon after they arrived, from separate worlds, at Boston College. It had started as a little joke between them, when Marcel had cast a sly smile at Charles during a lecture on the French and Indian Wars. Their alliance was a conspiracy against history, a challenge to the end of the Seven Years' War. By fate the two men had the same French surname, and this fate is perhaps the reason why they were assigned to share a room in the men's hall. Roommates for the past three years, now the

pair spent their Christmas holiday virtually alone on the grounds in Boston. Neither could return to his own country.

Charles's name was borrowed from the Jesuit fathers. From them he had adapted his tongue to French and Latin and the Eucharist, and as each of these alien tastes had dissolved in his mouth, he felt hungry for more. The first foreign languages came a little easier to him than English. For Marcel, it was much the same—first he spoke his mother tongue, then Latin, then English. When the two friends needed to speak most easily to one another they fell into French. But Charles remained always alone in his own first language.

In their quiet room, Charles fixed his eyes on the front page. A FIGHT WITH THE HOSTILES. BIG FOOT'S TREACHERY PRECIPITATES A BATTLE.

Marcel groaned softly as he allowed his body to collapse onto his bed. Marcel stared at the ceiling. The familiarity of this repose provided him some comfort, as he gave his mind to thoughts of his father. In August Marcel had begged his parents to allow him to stay home in Paris, to help his mother run the bookstore after the stroke. But Marcel's father had insisted that his son return to his studies. Now Marcel could think only of his need to hear his father's voice again.

Marcel wasn't sure if Charles had made a noise, or moved, or what precisely, but Marcel became aware of his friend. Marcel turned his face toward the desk.

The words came out dry and mechanical. "What is the news?" Marcel asked.

Charles did not answer right away.

Then Charles cleared his throat and held the paper away from his chest.

"There was a battle," he said.

Marcel sat up. "And?"

"Many were killed. It says here . . . "

Charles cleared his throat again.

"It says here that *Big Foot's braves turned upon their captors this morning and a bloody fight ensued. The trouble came when the soldiers attempted to disarm the Indians, who had surrendered to Major Whiteside. This move on the part of the troops was resisted, and a bloody and desperate battle at close quarters followed, in which the Indians were shot down ruthlessly and in which the lives of several soldiers were . . . sacrificed.*"

Charles paused. His eyes scanned the column. He continued: "*The Indians were shot down wherever found, no quarter being given by any one . . . It is doubted if by night either a buck or a squaw out of all Big Foot's band is left to tell the tale of this day's treachery.*"

Charles closed the paper and laid it to the side of his desk.

Charles shifted his body slightly away from his friend. He pulled open the desk drawer and extracted a small wooden box. He carefully withdrew a quillwork amulet attached to a leather cord. He ran his thumb across its gentle form, a little blue lizard.

"*Non*," Marcel whispered. "*Cela ne peut pas . . . *"

Charles nodded. He could not turn to his friend. Charles would not look at the mirror, the door, the bed. He could see only his mother's work in his hands.

Outside the snow continued to fall.

A rap on the door shook the stillness of the room. Both men looked up.

"Telegram!" came a voice from the other side.

Charles rose, crossed the room, and calmly opened the door. Marcel watched the black-rimmed paper pass from the dispatcher's hand to Charles. Marcel buried his face in his hands

and waited for Charles to deliver the news. But Charles did not come to Marcel's side.

Marcel heard a noise then, the crinkle of paper like the hush of a falling leaf. Marcel slowly turned his gaze to his friend. Immediately he saw why Charles had remained in place: the telegram was for him.

Fish Wars

My parents are fighting again. I pull the covers over my ears to try to muffle the sound, but my mother's whisper cuts through every layer and my father's voice seeps like water into a boat. They've been doing this lately. Fighting. But I can never quite hear what they are fighting about. I roll over and look at Jolene but she's sleeping like a log. Or she's faking it. Either way, it's easy for her to shut it out, since they aren't really her parents. I wonder if they will get a divorce.

I start to imagine them setting us down at the kitchen table and giving us the news. My little sister would bawl and say she wants to stay with our mom. And Lionel would say he's big enough to just move out on his own. Move in with his friends, 'cause he'll be eighteen in June anyway. Jolene would say she's going back to Alaska to find her dad. Mom would be sitting there, calm as a tree, but Dad would be cracking some joke and trying to make everyone laugh, and it would be killing me to think of my dad living all by himself. But what kind of girl doesn't pick her mom? And it would all come down to me: Do I stay with Mom or pick Dad?

Right in the middle of this I realize that something has happened. They stopped. I hold my breath. Then *pow*! I hear this loud thump and I think one of them has slammed something into the table. A fist, a coffee mug, a bowling ball. Okay, maybe not

a bowling ball, because that would probably be *really* loud. And nobody here bowls. So okay, that was stupid. No bowling ball. But something, *something* hit the table. And right after that I hear the door crank open and the sound of my dad's boots crushing gravel. Next sound (predictably): pickup-truck door. Then the Ford squeals because Dad twisted the key too hard in the ignition. Way to make an exit, Dad! The wheels scatter rock as he pulls out of the yard.

I wonder where he is going. Worse, I wonder what it will be like when he comes back.

Two weeks ago, I was at a slumber party at my friend Nicole's house. Nicole's family lives in town, not on the Rez, although there are plenty of white families like hers who live here. There were seven of us there, which turned out *not* to be such a lucky number. At first it was really fun, because Nicole's big sister Karen was watching us. She made us three Totino's pizzas and let us drink all the pop we wanted. I love Fresca, so I had some of that, and then Jolene and I split an Orange Crush. Karen was drinking Tab. She's the drill mistress at the high school, which means she (a) is in charge of the drill team, and (b) did not make cheerleader. She's still popular, though, even without being a cheerleader. And she was really nice to us, and showed us how to do a French manicure. Turns out it's easier than it looks.

After dinner we go downstairs to the rec room. We tell Karen we're going to listen to music and make crank calls. She seems cool with that. Lisa, a girl in my class, says she brought a surprise for us, and I think it's going to be candy bars or makeup. She gets her pillow, where she has stuffed her pajamas and toothbrush, and pulls out a record album: *Bill Cosby Is a Very Funny Fellow . . . Right!* I was *not* expecting that. More surprising is that when she opens it, there are two records in the sleeve: Bill Cosby and Dick

Gregory. I wonder if this is something white families do to store their albums. She looks kind of embarrassed and says her parents won't let her listen to that one. Nicole grabs it and puts it on. We listened to Dick Gregory, and at first we are all excited because we think there will be some dirty jokes. But there aren't any, just a lot of jokes about "Big Daddy" in Washington and the war and Cuba and how people in Minnesota have funny laws, like not allowing oleo. He said a lot of things I thought were pretty interesting. After it's over, Nicole says she wants the Cosby album, but everyone else (I guess me included) wants the radio. We turn the radio on and right away the Beach Boys come on, and everyone's pretty happy after that.

But then all this crazy stuff starts going down. We decide to do each other's hair, and we're listening to the radio, you know, it's all cool. "Louie Louie" comes on and Becky jumps up on the bed and starts singing and dancing. And right when she's singing, "Yeah yeah yeah yeah," and I mean *right at that minute*, with her mouth wide open, we hear someone pounding on the door upstairs. Then someone's loud feet stomp overhead, and we realize that there's a man up there, an unhappy man.

Two women are shouting at each other, and Nicole and Becky look at each other. The man is growling, too, and all these indistinct sounds blend together.

And then things go totally sideways.

Karen comes flying down the stairs and tells us it's okay, which is clearly a lie because we can hear Becky's mom screaming at Nicole's mom about stealing her man, Bruce. It's Bruce up there stomping around and yelling too. Karen puts her arms around Nicole, who is now having about the crappiest birthday party on record. And of course it's bad for Becky, too, because that's her dad up there with Nicole's mom, and her mom getting all crazy,

and it's not even her birthday or her house and no one knows what to do. Becky gets up and goes to the bathroom and shuts the door. No one is talking now, we're just sitting there, clutching our pillows and wishing we were asleep. Or just somewhere else. The radio is still on pretty loud, and "She Loves You" comes on, which I normally think is a happy song.

Anyhow, that is what happens at the birthday party. We all have to take sides, because after a while Becky's mom leaves and it gets quiet upstairs, and Karen goes to her room too. At this point Nicole and Becky can't even look at each other, and it seems like Becky is going to stay in the bathroom bawling all night. I try to help Becky feel better, and so does Jolene. So we end up never really getting any sleep.

In the morning Nicole's mom comes out in a big pink bathrobe and acts like nothing happened. She gives us cereal and she's real cheerful and nice. We don't see Bruce, but I see his crusty old work socks in the hallway and I wonder if he's there or if he snuck out early. I can't wait for my mom to come and get me and Jolene, so I ask to borrow the phone and call her. I don't usually think of our house as anything special, but I can't wait to get home.

Maybe it's just my imagination, but it seems like ever since that slumber party my parents have been fighting. And I hear them and I just hope that my dad isn't doing something like Becky's dad. One thing I know, though. If some woman stole my dad, my mom would *not* make a scene. She'd just put his stuff outside. That's what she always says: *If a man don't treat his family right, you put his stuff outside and he knows he can't come back. That's the old way.* I start thinking about this, and then I'm worried that maybe Mom is putting his stuff out *right now,* so I pull back the covers and walk slo-mo toward the door. It seems like every time I put my foot down the floor creaks, and even my breath sounds loud. I try

to control it all, breathe slow, go mountain-lion style to the door. I finally get there and turn the knob, and *jeez*, it sounds like a cow kicking a metal fence. My heart is beating fast and so dang *loud*, I can't tell what sounds are outside of me and what are in. By this time I'm wishing I had just stayed in bed, but now I'm too far out, and I can't catch a current to get back.

I sneak down the hallway and listen. Nothing. I stick my head around the arched entry to the living room, and I see her sitting there at the end of the sofa, reading a book. *Cat's Cradle.* I think I'm being super quiet, but she looks up at me, looks me right in the face. She puts the book down and whispers: *C'mere.* She opens her arms as I land on the sofa, and she asks me if I'm sick or can't sleep or what. I say *I don't know, I just can't sleep.* She tips me into her lap, and she strokes my hair and sings to me, the one she sang to me as a baby, with my name in the song:

> *Hush a-bye, don't you cry*
> *Go to sleep little Trudy*
> *When you awake, you will find*
> *All the pretty little horses*
> *Blacks and bays, dapples and grays*
> *All the pretty little horses*

I wake up in the morning on the couch with a green wool blanket over me. The house is quiet. Through the window, I can see my dad's truck in the drive. As everyone starts getting up, Dad comes out to the kitchen to make breakfast. He's whistling as he starts the coffee and pulls out a pan to cook eggs. Mom shuffles in, her eyes puffy. He pulls her to himself with a one-armed hug, and she rests her head for a second on his shoulder. I ask myself if this is normal. My eyes say yes, but my gut says no.

Things seem pretty quiet for the next few days. No late-night escapes for my dad, no puff-eyes from my mom. Then at breakfast one morning Dad says to Lionel, "You're not goin' to school today. I need you here." Lionel gets a huge smile on his face, and Jolene and I ask if we can stay home, too. Without looking at us, Dad says no and tells us to get our shoes on.

Since Lionel gets a hooky day, Mom walks us out to the bus stop at the end of our lane, which is about a quarter mile. The fog is thick and low on the ground, so we know the bus is going to be late. I ask Mom what kind of work Lionel is doing with Dad, and why we can't stay home, too. She says they're mending nets. And that we have to go to school. I think, *Okay, so there's no real reason why we have to go to school. Just that we do.* I make a loud sigh. I'm not satisfied, but I'm not going to sass. Pretty soon we see the lights of the bus cut through the fog, and that big yellow tank pulls up to our stop. Jolene hops on like it's the Tilt-A-Whirl at the Pierce County Fair, and my little sister, Janey, clings to Mom, also like it's the Tilt-A-Whirl at the fair. I peel her away, feeling like I'm the only one around here who sees things as they are.

When we get home, we walk past a string of pickups parked along the lane. I recognize most of them. We get to the yard, and I see all the men hanging out in the shed. There's Cecil and Uncle Billy and Frank and Dave. The door is propped open, and I can see them smoking and talking. Lionel is sitting there, too, listening. They are crowded around a space heater, wearing their work denims and flannel-lined jackets. Uncle Billy is talking. A big fish net is spread between them.

"What are they doing?" I ask.

Jolene shrugs. "Boring," she says.

Just then we hear a car creeping up the lane, and there's Grandma Wilma in her giant green Pontiac. She pulls up to the

house and we run to her. Janey gets her hugs in first, probably because she's littlest, and then Jolene, probably because she's adopted. When I get my turn, I give Grandma Wilma the biggest hug I can. She is barely bigger than me now, just a twig of an old lady, but her arms are like steel bands. I bet she could cream Jack Lalanne in a push-up contest. Nothing personal against Jack Lalanne.

Grandma Wilma brings out her sewing basket and we go inside. Auntie Rose is already there, drinking coffee with Mom. She tells us to get our beadwork out, and pretty soon everyone is pulling out their work and making a space on the table. Mom pours coffee for Grandma Wilma, and I show her my new moccasin pattern. We're just getting started and Grandma Twila shows up with apple spice cake, which is my favorite. I pretty much forget about anything that's going on in the shed, now that the beading ladies are around. They are always telling jokes and making everyone laugh, so I decide to try out some new material on them.

"You know, there are some pretty funny laws out there," I say.

"I don't know how *funny* they are," Grandma Wilma says, and we all laugh.

"Like in Minnesota," I say. "Do you know that in Minnesota it's illegal to buy oleo?"

They laugh again.

"Oleo!" I say, for effect. "You think they are selling it on the street? *Psssst*," I say, pretending to open my pretend jacket. "*You wanna buy some oleo?*"

They laugh again. "And you know the Supreme Court," I say.

"Oh, I know those guys," Grandma Twila says.

"Well, the Supremes say kids can't pray in school," I say. "So I want to know: How are we gonna pass our tests now?"

They just smile this time, and nod. So I try another tack.

"The teacher sees a bunch of boys in the back and says, 'Hey, you looking at dirty magazines?' And they say, 'Oh no, we're prayin'!'"

This gets more of a chuckle. I decide to try one more. "You know the South is bad for Negroes. But in North Dakota, all the white people are cool with them. You know why? 'Cause in North Dakota they got so many Indians around!"

They laugh again, but not the same way. I look at Mom and she's not laughing. Or even smiling. "Where do you hear these things?" she asks. "At school?"

Jolene looks up at me. Then she looks at Mom and says, "On a record."

I can't believe that Jolene just blew this whole thing for me. I give her the stink eye.

Mom's brow furrows. "What record?"

"Uh, Dick Gregory," I say. "He's a comedian. Like Bill Cosby."

Mom's face brightens a little, but she doesn't quite smile. "You're part right," she says, although I'm not sure what part she means.

Around dinnertime Jolene and I get sent to the kitchen to peel potatoes. Uncle Billy and Dave come in with Dad and Lionel, and Mom cooks a big hash of potatoes and smoked salmon for everyone. Mom and Dad seem pretty normal, and I'm thinking that they probably won't get a divorce. Becky's parents are definitely getting a divorce, and it looks like Becky and Nicole are going to be half-sisters or something like that soon, even though they can't stand each other. We eat the cake and do the dishes, then bedtime comes and everyone is still there. Dad tells us to go to bed. I think it's going to be hard to go to sleep, but instead I drift away like a cloud.

The next morning Grandma Wilma is in the kitchen. At first, I'm not sure what's going on. I feel like maybe I'm not awake. Jolene is right behind me. She says, "Hi, Grandma," like she's there every day. I'm starting to think Jolene and Grandma Wilma are related. I wonder if Grandma Wilma has spent the night. She's making flapjacks, wearing the exact same clothes she had on yesterday. She says good morning and sends Jolene back to the bedroom to make sure Janey is getting herself dressed. She tells me to set the table.

"Where's Mom?" I ask, opening the cabinet.

"She's taking care of some things," she says from the griddle.

I look at the stack of plates.

"How many plates?" I ask.

She thinks for a minute. "Four."

Four. That's me, Jolene, Janey, and Lionel. Or me, Jolene, Janey, and Dad. Or me, Jolene, Janey, and Grandma Wilma. I leave the stack of plates on the counter and run to Lionel's room. I don't knock like I'm supposed to, I just push the door open and it's still as the moon in there. His bed, with the blue star quilt, is still made. There's not a wrinkle on it.

"Where's Lionel?" I yell down the hall.

But Grandma Wilma is right there. She moves like a cat.

"Did Lionel go to the Army?" I ask.

"Trudy," she says, and I feel the curve of her hand gently close on my bicep. She steers me toward the kitchen. "Lionel's with your folks. They just asked me to get you girls to school this morning." We walk down the hall in awkward silence. "Everything is going to be okay," she says.

I stop and look Grandma Wilma in the face. "What do you mean, everything's *going* to be okay?"

I'm afraid she'll think I'm giving her sass, but her expression doesn't change. As she's looking at me, I notice for the first time that her dark eyes are rimmed with gray, almost blue on the edges. *Everything is okay*, she says. I realize that Jolene and Janey are standing there watching this whole drama, and I decide to buck up.

I nod. I look over at my sisters. "Everything's fine," I say. Jolene shrugs. Janey nods earnestly and repeats, "It's okay."

"Good," Grandma Wilma says. "Now set the table."

Grandma Wilma makes the best flapjacks, but I have a feeling that any day that starts with half your family AWOL is not going to go right. At school, we get off the bus and Jolene and I are walking to the fifth-grade yard when I hear some boy yelling at me.

"Hey, Trudy," he yells. "Trudy John!"

I follow the voice and it's coming from a pack of sixth-grade boys. Is it a pack? I'm not sure that's the right word. There are three of them, maybe not enough for what you normally might consider a pack. But it's really the way they move. They move like a pack, and they are drifting toward me and Jolene. I wonder why they're breaking Rule No. 1 of the Unspoken Code of the Playground: sixth graders *never* talk to fifth graders. I'm surprised they even know my name.

"Hey, Tru-dee," comes from the mouth of the skinny buzz-cut boy in the middle, Dale Davis. He's wearing Wrangler jeans and a dingy white T-shirt, no jacket, even though it's only fifty degrees out and a cold wind is skidding off the bay.

"What," I say.

"Saw your dad today."

A crow flaps over to a tree beside us and caws from her branch: *A-ah, a-ah.*

"Yep," Dale says, rocking back slightly on his heels, his hands stuffed in the front pockets of his jeans. "Saw your mom too. Down at the PD."

For a second I feel scared. For a second I think he might know something, because his dad is a state bull.

"Liar," Jolene says.

"Yeah," I say. "Liar."

His skinny face contracts. He tips his head, squints up in the tree at the crow. *A-ah, a-ah.* "Nope," Dale says. "Pretty dang sure that was your mom bailing your dad's ass out of jail this morning. I figure he was drunk."

"Shut up," I say.

Dale lunges forward, then staggers to the side. He stops, and mimes drinking like he's got a bottle in his hand. "Look at me," he says, and staggers around some more. "I'm a drunk Indian! Get me some firewater!" His friends laugh. He stumbles around like a lame man walking through sand.

SHUT UP, I yell.

Dale straightens. "Not my fault your dad's a drunk," he says.

And that's when I snap, going at him like a whale butting a boat. I go straight for his belly, throw myself into him, and knock him to the ground. That asphalt comes to meet me fast, and I feel the impact of falling down with him. Breath gets knocked out of us both. I scramble to stay on top of him. I feel the tense muscle of his open hand crash into my nose and a pain so sharp I don't know whether to cry or throw up. My eyes are closed and I'm throwing my hands at his face, not even sure if I'm making a fist. I hear someone yelling *fight fight* and *a-ah, a-ah* and then he tips me off of him and I land on my back while he jumps up.

This is how Mrs. Bartholomew finds us. I see blood on my hand, a bright streak across the knuckles, before I realize I've

got blood all over my jacket and front. I can feel it now pouring out of my nose and I swallow big globs of it down my throat as Mrs. Bartholomew pulls me up by the elbow. She tilts my head and squeezes my nose with a hankie, which hurts like heck, and tells me to hold it until the bleeding stops. Of course we're not wasting any time getting to the principal's office so I have to walk and apply direct pressure at the same time. Jolene is right there, holding my arm to guide me, and Mrs. Bartholomew has Dale by the shoulder. His friends have split. I guess it wasn't a pack after all. She marches him straight to the office, and tells Jolene to take me to the school nurse.

As the nurse cleans me up I try to make it seem not so bad. "You should see the other guy," I say. "He's got even *more* of my blood on him." The nurse gives a little smile and Jolene laughs, because she knows it's true. The nurse checks my nose and says it isn't broken, just bruised, and gives me aspirin for the pain.

Jolene waits with me in the nurse's room while the principal calls my mom.

"Are you scared?" she asks.

"A little," I say.

"Don't be scared," she says.

"I think I'm getting suspended."

"It's not bad," she says. "Everyone talks about it like it's bad, but it's just a couple days of no school."

"Were you ever suspended?"

"Not really," she says, and I wonder what she could possibly mean. It seems like more of a yes-or-no question. After a minute she says, "When I lived with my mom, sometimes I didn't go to school. I stayed at home. Sometimes it felt strange, but then I would find things to do."

"Were you by yourself?"

"Yeah," she says. "Mostly. But that was back in first and second grade. A long time ago."

She looks down at her hands and decides to pick at a hangnail. I want to know more, but I can't ask. Jolene has lived with us since we were both eight. Her mom is my dad's older sister, and Dad drove to the train depot in Seattle to pick up Jolene when she came down from Alaska, all by herself, after her mom went to prison. I remember the first time I saw Jolene coming up the walk with Dad. She was wearing a white anorak with a fur-trimmed hood and a pair of mukluks her grandma had made for her. Her face was skinny and fierce, all hard angles and beauty, like the carved talisman of walrus tusk that she keeps in her sock drawer.

I know for a fact that the day Jolene came to live with us was the day my dad gave up drinking forever. Not that he was much of a drinker to start with, not like some folks. He mostly would just drink when his buddies came over. They would go out to the shed and smoke and drink beers and talk about Korea. He drank other times too, I guess. Well Jolene comes and I guess Dad figures that he's all she's got now, or we're all she's got now, and he quits. I wonder if he will come to the principal's office. Or if my mom will come. Or Grandma Wilma.

One thing I know for sure: my dad's not a drunk.

I think about this and I get riled at Dale Davis all over again. *Jerk!* My entire face is throbbing.

After a while the door opens, and the nurse says my mom is here, and Jolene can go back to her class. Jolene asks if she can please stay with me, but the nurse tells her no. Jolene slips through the door without looking back, but I tell her *thanks* and *see you at home* as she leaves.

Mom is standing in the hallway outside of the principal's office, looking out the window at the empty playground. *Mom,* I say,

and she turns her face toward me. A look of surprise, then maybe anger, ripple across her face. I feel small. She opens her arms and hugs me, then pulls back and scans my face and jacket.

"Will it come out?" I ask.

She frowns a little. "We'll see," she says. "We'll try."

She hugs me again. "Are you okay?"

That's when I start to cry. I wonder why moms can make you cry when you don't know you have to. *Where were you?* I ask. *In town,* she says. She fishes a tissue out of her pocket and puts her arm around me as we walk to the car. She sits in the car with me at the school while the story falls out of my mouth in rough little pieces. I cry so hard my nose starts to bleed again. She's out of tissues, so she grabs one of Lionel's jersey work gloves that's lying on the car seat and catches the blood with it. It smells like sweat and car-engine oil, which means it smells like Lionel. I hold it to my face with my head tipped back as she drives us home.

Turns out I'm suspended for a day, and that jerk Dale is out for the rest of the week, which is only three days, but still. At least he got it a little worse than me.

We get home and I think Mom will tell me what's going down but she doesn't. She calls her friend Janet and makes some coffee, then takes my jacket and sweater to the sink to wash the blood out. I stand next to her in the kitchen.

"Mom," I say. "I was scared when you weren't here."

She doesn't stop scrubbing the collar. Watery brown suds cling to her fingernails. "Um-hmm," she says. "But you shouldn't be afraid when Grandma Wilma is here. You should know that."

She turns on the faucet to rinse.

"When . . . when can you tell me where you were?"

"When your dad gets back."

This cannot be good. In my mind I see them setting us down

at the table, and I realize how much I don't want this to happen. The words just tumble out of my mouth then.

"Are you and Dad getting a divorce?"

She stops working and looks at me, a hard look.

"No," she says. "Of course not."

And then she tells me where she was: Pierce County Jail. We sit down at the table and she says Dad and Lionel were arrested last night. For fishing. For fishing on our river, where we have always fished. The game wardens caught them. Took their nets. Took them to jail. Mom paid a fine to get them out. As she's talking, different pictures spin through my mind. Dad's truck. The nets. Lionel's empty room. Apple spice cake. She says we're in this now, that the Indians got to fight. Just like the old days. I want her to say what Grandma Wilma says, that everything is going to be okay. But she doesn't.

I'm sitting on the sofa watching TV when Lionel, Jolene, and Janey come home. There's no need to explain my puffy face, since news like that goes 'round like fire. Lionel says my face looks bad.

"It *feels* like a baseball mitt," I say.

"Your face is purple," Jolene says. "Are you sure it isn't broken?"

"No," I say. "But there's nothing to do anyway. Not like I can put a cast on it." Janey laughs, and then I do, too, picturing me with a cast on my face. Lionel says he didn't know I wanted out of school so bad I'd get suspended for it.

"What about you?" I ask. "You went to jail."

He grins at that.

I tell him I was afraid that he'd run off to the Army. *Nah,* he says, *I'd go Navy like Dad.* I tell him that isn't very comforting, and he shrugs.

After dinner we watch Dad and Lionel get their boots and

coats on. Dad goes out and lays a net in the bed of the truck, and Lionel gets in the cab. Mom brings them a thermos of coffee. She stands on the front porch watching them. My coat is still wet, so I wrap myself in the green blanket off the sofa and go out. The sky is deep blue and still. The stars are awake. Dad waves at us, then the cab door snaps shut. We watch the truck creep down the drive, then turn onto the highway.

I sense my mom turning her face away from the road, away from the glow of red taillights, now disappeared in the dark. We look at the sky together. She points and says, *There they are.* She is pointing at the fish traps. Her voice is flat and matter-of-fact. There they are. Nisqually fishing weirs. I look too. In school we've learned that these stars are called Orion and Orion's Belt. I nod, I don't speak. The stars to me seem cold and jagged and far, far away.

ʔiná·tx̣y̓aksa

I tell my story

I conjure my powers

I make a wish

Beading Lesson

The first thing you do is, lay down all your hanks, like this, so the colors go from light to dark, like a rainbow. I'll start you out with something real easy, like I do with those kids over at the school, over at Cay-Uma-Wa.

How about—you want to make some earrings for your mama? Yeah, I think she would like that.

Hey niece, you remind me of those kids. That's good! That's good to be thinking of your mama.

You go ahead and pick some colors you think she would like. Maybe three or four is all, and you need to pick some of these bugle beads.

Yeah, that's good, except you got too many dark colors.

You like dark colors. Every time I see you you're wearin' something dark. Not me. I like to wear red and yellow, so people know I'm around and don't try talkin' about me behind my back, aay?

The thing is, you got to use some light colors, because you're makin' these for your mama, right, and she has dark hair, and you want 'em to stand out, and if they're all dark colors, you can't see the pattern.

I got some thread for you, and this beeswax. You cut the thread about this long, a little longer than your arm, but you don't want it too long or it will tangle up or get real weak. You run

it through the beeswax, like this, until it's just about straight. It makes it strong and that way it don't tangle so much.

You keep all this in your box now. I got this for you to take home with you, back to college, so you can keep doin' your beadwork.

How do you like it over there at the university? You know your cousin Rae is just about gettin' her degree. She just has her practicum, then she'll be done. I think her boyfriend don't like her being in school though, and that's slowing her down. It's probably a good thing you don't have a boyfriend right now. They can really make a lot of trouble for you, and slow you down on things you got to do.

Now you gotta watch this part. This is how you make the knot. You make a circle like this, then you wrap the thread around the needle three times, see? You see how my hands are? If you forget later, you just remember how my hands are, just like this, and remember you have to make a circle, okay? Then you pull the needle through all the way to the end—good—and clip off the little tail.

I'll show you these real easy earrings, the same thing I always start those men at the jail with. You know I go over there and give them beading lessons. You should see how artistic some of them are. They work real hard, and some of them are good at beadwork.

I guess they got a lot of time to do it, but it's hard, it's hard to do real good beadwork.

You got to go slow and pay attention.

I know this one man, William, he would be an artist if he wasn't in jail. I'll show you, he gave me a drawing he did of an eagle. It could be a photograph, except you can tell it's just pencil. But it's good, you would like it. There's a couple of other Indian

prisoners—I guess we're supposed to call them inmates, but I always call them prisoners—and sometimes I make designs for them for their beadwork from what they draw. The thing is, they don't get many colors to work with.

They like the beadwork, though. They always got something to give their girlfriends when they come visit, or their mothers and aunties.

You have to hide the knot in the bead, see, like this, and that's why you got to be careful not to make the knot too big.

Maybe next time you come they will be having a powwow at the prison and you can meet my students over there and they can show you their beadwork. I think they always have a pow-wow around November, around Veterans Day. Your cousin Carlisle and his family come over from Montana last time, and the only thing is, you got to go real early because it takes a long time to get all your things through security. They have to check all your regalia and last time they almost wouldn't let Carlisle take his staff in because they said it was too dangerous or something.

What's that? Oh, that's all right. Just make it the same way on the other one and everyone will think you did it that way on purpose.

Your mama is really going to like those earrings. I think sometimes she wishes she learnt to bead, but she didn't want to when she was little. She was the youngest, so I think she was a little spoiled but don't tell her I said that. She didn't have to do things she didn't want to, she didn't even have to go to boarding school. I think she would have liked it. It wasn't bad for me at that school. Those nuns were good to me; they doted on me. I was their pet. I think your mama missed out on something, not going to St. Andrew's, because that's when you get real close with other Indians.

I like that blue. I think I'm goin' to make you a wing dress that color.

I think you'll look good when you're ready to dance. Once you get going on your beadwork I'll get you started on your moccasins, and you know your cousin Woody is making you a belt and I know this lady who can make you a cornhusk bag. You're goin' to look just like your mama did when she was young, except I think she was younger than you the last time she put on beadwork.

I used to wonder if you would look like your dad, but now that you're grown you sure took after her. I look at you and I think my sister, she must have some strong blood.

Hey, you're doin' real good there, niece. I think you got "the gift"—good eyesight! You know, you always got to be workin' on something, because people are always needing things for weddin's and memorials and going out the first time, got to get their outfits together. Most everything I make I give away, but people pay me to make special things. And they are always askin' for my work at the gift shop. My beadwork has got me through some hard times, some years of livin' skinny.

You got to watch out for some people, though. Most people aren't like this; most people are real bighearted. But some people, when they buy your beadwork, they think it should last forever. Somebody's car breaks down, he knows he got to take it to the shop, pay someone to get it goin' again. But not with beadwork— not with something an Indian made. No, they bring it back ten years later and they want you to fix it for free! They think because an Indian makes it, it's got to last forever. Just think if the Indians did that with all the things the government made for us. Hey, you got to fix it for free!

You done with that already? Let me show you how you finish.

You pull the thread through this line, see, then clip it, then the bead covers it up. That's nice.

That's good. I'm proud of you, niece.

I think your mama is really goin' to like these earrings, and maybe she'll come and ask you to teach her how you do it. You think she'll ever want to do beadwork? Maybe she'll come and ask me, aay?

What do you think of that? You think your mama would ever want to learn something from her big sister? I got a lot of students. There's a lady who just called me the other day, she works at the health clinic, and she's older than you and she wants to learn how. I said sure I'll teach her. I teach anyone who wants to learn. I just keep thinkin' if I stay around long enough, everyone's goin' to come back and ask me, even your mama.

wIndin!

THE EXHILARATING GAME OF KINSHIP,
CHANCE & ECONOMIC REDISTRIBUTION
AGES 5 AND UP
HIGH PLATEAU EDITION

OBJECT. The object of *wIndin!* is to host the most Give Aways and thus secure your status as having the most money, trade goods, kinship relations, and honor. The winner must successfully avoid having part or all of his or her assets taken into trust by the federal government.

PREPARATION. Unfold the circular board and place it on a flat surface. Place the deck of Stick Game cards facedown on the blanket icon in the central area of the board. Distribute five horses to each player, placing extra horses in the Agency corral. Distribute five Pendleton Blanket cards to each player, placing the remaining cards on the Longhouse icon. Leave the TRUST PIT empty.

—

Each player selects a token to travel around the board. The tokens are moccasin, diggin' stick, cowboy hat, dip net, headdress, cornhusk bag, and giant beaded belt buckle.

"Indian tokens or token Indians?"

"Definitely Indian tokens."

Iris nodded and typed quickly on her MacBook. Trevor was washing dishes in the sink, and for a short interlude the only sound between them was the regular rhythm of plates moving under sponge and water. "Wait," she said. "That won't work. Because then all of the Indians will be saying, 'I want to be the Indian.'"

"No, it'd be like, 'I want to be THE INDIAN.'"

"Then you're back to the token Indian."

Trevor stopped washing.

"Okay, screw the token Indians," he said. "You need a BIA Agent or something. An anthropologist."

"That is so cliché. How about just some guy in a suit, writing in a little notebook? Then it could be ambiguous."

"Ambiguous!" Trevor pulled the drain and wiped his sudsy hands on a towel. In three efficient steps he was at the table, looking over her shoulder at the screen. "A guy in a suit is totally FBI."

"Hmmm. I'm not feeling it." Iris tapped her fingers on the table and stared at the fruit bowl.

"Give him a giant notebook and tiny, tiny hands."

"I don't know, Trev."

"C'mon. You want to leave out the G-man? Where's the fun in that?"

"It's too *Thunderheart.*"

"Fine! Play the Val Kilmer card," Trevor said, extracting a chair from the table with a loud scrape on the floor. "Just kill my idea." He sat down.

"No, wait. We *should* have a Val Kilmer card—you know, you draw a Stick Game card and it says, 'You have just sighted Val Kilmer in South Dakota. Pay each player ten dollars.'"

"Fuck that. They should pay you. Twenty bucks. For restitution."

Iris typed quickly, her eyes fixed on the screen. She had only a few months to finish her project, a piece of installation art for the annual Indian Art Northwest show in Portland over Memorial Day.

Trevor picked up a piece of fruit from the bowl on the table and polished its skin on his shirt. He held it out to her.

"Hey," he said. "How about this?"

Her fingers grazed his thumb as she reached for the apple and lifted it from his hand. "Don't be mean," she said, and took a bite.

EQUIPMENT. This game is played on a circular board. It includes a single die, eight player tokens, a set of Pendleton Blanket cards, a set of Appaloosa tokens, a set of Stick Game cards, and play money.

MONEY. The bank is maintained by the Tribal Chair, who volunteers for the position and/or is elected by the other players and/or claims hereditary descent. Each player is given $2,000 in any

combination of fifties, twenties, and tens that the Tribal Chair determines. The Tribal Chair is expected to keep *wIndin!* funds separate from his or her personal funds, unless he or she draws the Tribal Corruption card from among the Stick Game cards. The Corruption card is a trump card that allows the Chair to raid the bank and steal horses with impunity.

The first time Iris had seen Trevor, she was standing at the window of her second-floor apartment building and he was waiting at the bus stop on the street corner below. It wasn't really her habit to stand at the window, but on that day she was watering the ficus and happened to look out and see him. It was September, more than a year ago, and the maple leaves were just beginning to flame. When she saw the beautiful man at the bus stop, her heart quickened: the long, straight legs, vaguely thick middle, broad shoulders, and black hair. Still, she couldn't be sure; her view was admittedly limited. She crouched down below the sill, peeking over the edge to watch him. The bus approached, and he turned toward it. In profile, she made a positive ID: Yakama! The Pendleton shoulder bag clinched it.

That was back in the day when Iris had first moved to Eugene, the small university town that nonetheless seemed big to her. She had landed a job building websites and print publications at Design Depot, an all-service copy shop, after working for two years as the internet specialist for the *Confederated Umatilla Journal*. She had an associate's degree from Blue Mountain Community College, and she occasionally thought about going back to college, perhaps for a BFA. Her sparsely furnished living room was dominated by a wall of family photos intermingled with prints and

photographs of works by her favorite artists: Marcus Amerman, Shelley Niro, David Bradley, T. C. Cannon, and Diego Romero.

After Iris spied Trevor at the bus stop, she began to track the mass-transit ridership more carefully. She parked her green Toyota Corolla behind her apartment building. She spotted Trevor a few more times and once rode the same bus with him. These nonencounters finally came to an end when she saw him at the Longhouse, for a potluck on Indigenous Peoples' Day (or *Columbus Day in Drag*, as Iris called it, although who was she to mess with the politics of urban Indians?). As Iris and Trevor were roughly the same age—midtwenties—they folded into the buffet line at the same time. Just as they were shuffling past the salads, a fresh platter of roasted salmon emerged from the kitchen.

"Stand back," Trevor said. "You don't want to get caught between the elders and the salmon cheeks."

Iris laughed. "You know the most dangerous place? Between Russell Means and a camera."

There was a pause, then a laugh. And from that moment on they were friends.

TO PLAY. All tokens are placed on the Home space, identified by the continental map of North America. To begin play, each player rolls the die. The first to roll a five begins, and the play proceeds from player to player in a clockwise fashion. Each player takes a turn by throwing the die and moving the corresponding number of spaces. If a player lands on a casino, he or she has the option to roll again but is not obligated to do so. More than one token can occupy a space at any given time, in accordance with special treaty provision.

—

PROTOCOL. Players are expected to respect the integrity of the circle and never move their tokens across the board, but rather proceed always in a circular fashion. Protocol must be monitored by all players at the table. Breaking protocol can result in arbitrary fines, family shame, and teasing by other players.

In the time that Trevor and Iris had known each other, they had been through a fair share of dramas together. Like most young Indians, they were preoccupied with their social lives, family situations, and the perennial question of going to law school. Every Indian family pressures its children to do something useful, and law school inevitably presents itself as a path to this end. Iris felt no particular aptitude for federal Indian law, despite her congenital familiarity with it, but Trevor had been struck with the fever in the fifth grade when he saw Al Smith at a powwow. As Al Smith circled around the arena, visiting and joking with small clusters of Indians, Trevor would hear folks whisper in his wake: "There's Al Smith!" and "That's Al Smith!" Trevor wondered what astonishing powers this slight man with the long graying braids might possess. Trevor strolled over to the bleachers and asked his uncle, "Who is Al Smith?" Trevor's uncle had scanned the crowd, then pointed with his chin. "That's Al Smith." Trevor sighed, then asked again: "What did he *do*?" Trevor's uncle leaned back against the wooden bleacher and regarded his nephew. Finally the uncle said, "You ever hear of *Smith v. Oregon*? That's Al Smith. He's the one who fought for us all the way to the Supreme Court."

Trevor's uncle explained that Al Smith had been fired for taking peyote during a Native American Church ceremony, and that the State had then denied Smith unemployment benefits, saying that Smith had been fired for misconduct. Smith defended himself on the grounds of religious freedom and lost.

Trevor's uncle shook his head slightly. Then he went on: "You know who did that? Scalia! The Catholic! I tell you, we should fire that Scalia on Monday for taking Communion on Sunday." Trevor's uncle paused. "Al Smith fought for us," he said, "and Congress tried to fix what the Court done. We have some religious protections because of him." Trevor sat silently and thought about the story his uncle had told him. He looked out across the arena, and he felt his heart surge when he saw *Al Smith v. Oregon* standing beside a drum, laughing.

When Trevor went to the university, he majored in history and political science, dutifully treading his path toward a JD. On the morning that Iris had first seen Trevor, in fact, he was on his way to his LSAT preparation course. As it happened, Trevor was also on his way to falling in love with his LSAT instructor, Brian, who would later dump him the night before the appointed test date. Consequently, on the morning of the exam Trevor was still so drunk that his hangover hadn't even started, giving him just the sense of invincibility he needed to propel him forward. He got up and drank a glass of water. It had a slight aftertaste of irony. He pondered his options. He had to move on. He summoned all the warrior strength he'd learned from his mother and delivered himself to the testing site, the wound sitting in his chest as numb and rubbery as an eraser.

TO ROAM. Once play begins, players are expected to continue around the board in turn. Exceptions to this rule are the

following: (1) When a player's token lands on any of the following spaces: Home, Julyamsh, Pendleton Round-Up, Crow Fair, Pi-Uma-Sha Treaty Days, Gathering of Nations, or the Intertribal Friendship House. On these spaces, the player has the option to pass and will not be required to roll the die and move until the next round. (2) Alternatively, a player has the option to roll again and thus accelerate forward movement around the board, i.e., Get Out of Dodge.

HOME. Each time that a player circles back to Home, the player will receive the following combination of cash and trade goods: one hundred dollars from the bank; one hundred dollars from the player to his or her right; a horse from the corral; and a Pendleton Blanket card. For each Give Away that the player has hosted on that particular circle around the board, the allocation of cash and trade goods will be doubled. Players are not awarded cash and trade goods simply for passing Home, but must actually land on Home to receive his or her allotted share. A player who draws a Get Back Home Free card from the Stick Game deck is allowed to redeem it at any time.

Iris had been there to pick up the pieces, so to speak. When the breakup was fresh, she regularly cooked for Trevor: noodle casseroles and meatloaf with potatoes, in huge quantities because that was the only way she knew how to make them. She stayed up late with him watching Jim Jarmusch movies. They went out drinking together, and she would ration one pint through the entire evening so that she could reasonably drive him home. She was careful about drinking anyway because she was quite small, with

a birdlike body: thin legs and a compact middle. Her face was round and sweet, framed by her squarish, red eyeglasses and spiky dark hair. Iris became very protective of Trevor during this time, conscripting herself to defend him against Brian's possible return. She knew that Brian occasionally phoned, and Trevor was always a wreck afterward.

Iris's job would have been easier, she thought, if she didn't like Brian. She was vigilant precisely because she could see why Trevor loved him. Brian had a sharp wit but he didn't use it unkindly, and he could make fun of himself. He was a generous partner to Trevor when they were together. But Brian had seemed too polite with Trevor, and it spoke of a peculiar distance that existed between them. Brian knew that he was the one more loved.

Keeping watch over Trevor's affections was the kind of distraction Iris needed that spring. Her auntie had been fighting off diabetes for years when one day a heart attack threw her to her knees in the produce aisle of the Safeway. Iris had gone straight home and stayed for two weeks, appointed at bedside, doing Design Depot assignments on her laptop while her auntie recovered from bypass surgery. When Iris had returned to her little apartment in Eugene, Trevor had been waiting at the door with a six-pack of Miller and an empty March Madness bracket.

"I can't do this without you," he said.

Inside the apartment, Trevor cracked open the beers. He set the bracket aside as Iris recounted the days with her family. Sometimes tears would spill out of her eyes while she was talking. She said that her auntie had dreamed of eels, and Iris knew that this meant that her auntie would live.

Trevor and Iris sat side by side on the couch that was so worn down that they slid together into the well of cushions in the

middle. Iris snuggled in to Trevor, and he lifted his arm to place it around her shoulder. His body was warm and reassuring.

"How have you been?" she asked.

He sighed.

"Brian?"

"Yeah," he said. "I just saw him in the parking lot of the store."

"It will get better," she said, patting his knee gently.

"My love life would be so much easier if I were white. And straight. And thin. And easy," he said. "Or just any one of those things."

"Don't be so hard on yourself," she said. "A little man belly is very attractive."

"Look, no offense," he said. "But straight women have lower expectations. The man belly isn't going to cut it in my world."

She pulled away from him a bit. She tried to push his last two words out of her mind, but they remained planted in her heart, a stubborn root.

FEASTS. Four Feast Days appear on the board. They are Root Feast, Salmon Feast, Huckleberry Feast, and Friendship Feast. When a player lands on a feast day, the player should exchange equivalent cash and/or trade goods with all other players (e.g., a horse for a horse, a blanket for a blanket, a twenty for a twenty). Players may negotiate for alternate exchanges as long as they are deemed equitable by both parties.

It was Columbus Day, so the buses were running on a holiday schedule, making public transit both slower and more crowded

than usual. When Iris finally climbed aboard, she was relieved to see Trevor standing toward the back, clutching the bar above for balance. She weaved into position next to him, wrapping her arm around the pole in the middle.

"Hey," she said.

"Ya-hey," he said. "I called in sick today."

"So what are you doing?" she asked.

"Going to the mall to celebrate the arrival of capitalism in the Americas." The bus made a tight turn and Iris struggled for balance, leaning momentarily into Trevor.

"I feel like I'm talking into your armpit," she said. Trevor switched arms. "Better?" he asked. It was. He asked how the work on *wIndin!* was going.

"I have this idea," she said. "I'm going to make a space called 'Racism-Free Zone,' but it is going to be too small to actually fit on."

"Cool," he said. The bus turned again, and he swayed in her direction. "Are you going to have a Jail?" he asked.

"No."

"Why not? Everyone is going to expect a jail. 'Go to Jail, go directly to Jail, do not pass Go, do not collect two hundred dollars—you know, something like that."

"No."

"Not even a low-security prison?"

"No."

"C'mon. You could make a card that says: 'Hey, Indians really *do* pay taxes! But not you, so the IRS is throwing your brown ass in the slam.'"

Iris sighed. She shifted position. He continued: "How about House Arrest? Just an ankle monitor."

"Trevor, that is effed up. No Indian has ever even seen a

low-security prison," she said. "No Indian has ever worn an ankle monitor."

"But it's not *real*. It's a game."

She looked up at him then, sudden and fierce. "I mean, it's *art*," he said. "It's political art."

"Right," she said. "I'm not having a jail."

STICK GAME CARDS. When a player lands on a Stick Game space, he or she must draw the top card from the deck of Stick Game cards, dispense or receive money and/or trade goods as the card indicates, and return the card to the bottom of the deck. The following exceptions apply: (1) A player may hold, trade, or sell the Tribal Corruption card once it has been drawn, and the holder of the card may retain it for the entire game. (2) If a player draws a Trust Pit card, the card must be taken out of circulation along with the player's cash assets and placed in the TRUST PIT in the middle of the board.

GIVE AWAY. There are three Give Away spaces on the board: Naming Give Away, Weddin' Give Away, and Memorial Give Away. When a player arrives on a Give Away space, he or she is expected to distribute horses, blankets, and cash to fellow players. The exact quantity of items is determined by the player; however, each player must be awarded some combination of cash and trade goods. In the event that a player who lands on a Give Away space does not have adequate resources to host a Give Away, the other players will make contributions to the host. Each player should maintain a record of Give Aways hosted, as the player who has the most Give Aways is declared the winner.

—

For Halloween, Trevor convinced Iris to go with him to a couples masquerade party as the Lone Ranger and Tonto. The party was a free-for-all, attracting the city's trendiest straight couples to the city's only gay bar. For a long time, Iris balked. But then Trevor played his trump card: What if Brian were there? So she gave in, and they found a white Western shirt at St. Vinny's for two dollars fifty cents, which went along with Iris's white denim pants, red cowboy boots, and black mask. Trevor, who had spent the summer working out, was showing off his newly svelte form in a body-conscious faux-buckskin outfit with laces up the front. When Iris caught a glimpse of herself with him in the glass storefronts that lined the sidewalk, she flushed for a moment with the thought that they could pass as a couple.

So Iris was surprised when she ran into an acquaintance in the restroom, a young woman who worked as a barista at the coffee shop next to Design Depot. The woman, Jill, was wearing a red miniskirt, white knee socks with patent black Mary Janes, and a red hooded cloak.

"Nice costume," Iris offered, lifting her mask. The elastic cord held it firmly to the top of her head.

Jill nodded brightly and removed her hood. "Thanks," she said, smoothing her thick brown hair with one hand. "Love your Lone Ranger look. You look so little next to Tonto."

"As it should be," Iris said. Jill gave a little laugh, showing her gleaming white teeth.

"So," Jill said. "Want to look in my basket?"

"Um, sure."

Jill took a step closer and pulled back the top. It was full of condoms.

"Good thinking," Iris said.

"It's my job to hand these out tonight. I'm volunteering for HIV Alliance." She offered the open basket to Iris. "Would you like one? Or five?"

Iris blushed suddenly and stepped back. "Uh, no thanks."

"So," Jill said. "You're not with that guy?" When Iris didn't answer, Jill continued, hurriedly: "I didn't think so—you don't really seem like a couple. I mean, except for the Lone Ranger–Tonto thing. Is he—is he your brother? I hope you don't mind me saying this, but he is really hot! Do you think you might be able to, you know, introduce us?"

In the rush of words Iris's gaze fixed on the gaping jaw of the basket, hanging open off Jill's arm.

"Sure," Iris said. Then added, "He'd be into you."

Jill thanked Iris and turned to the mirror to apply a fresh layer of lipstick. "See you out there!" she called as Iris left the room.

Iris drifted back to the table and saw that Trevor had ordered another round of beers. She sat down stiffly beside him. Trevor glanced at her.

"This sucks," she said.

Trevor leaned toward her ear. "What?" he asked, in a voice loud enough to prevail over the pounding techno beat.

"This girl in the women's room, she wants to meet you," Iris shouted back. Trevor shrugged his shoulders dismissively. "So?" he asked.

"It's not . . . " Iris struggled with her thoughts. "It's just . . . she acted like . . . " Iris caught her breath roughly. "She acted like there's no way someone like you would be with someone like me."

"Well, she's kind of right about that."

"But that's just it! She doesn't get that you're gay. She wants to hook up with you." Trevor registered her feelings and placed

his hand gently on her shoulder. A tear slipped and glided down her cheek. He looked intently at her. He lifted his hand from her shoulder and brushed her cheek.

"C'mon, Iris," he said. She swallowed hard against a wave of emotion.

"It's true," she said. "You're hot and I'm just . . . " Her voice trailed off. She felt absurd in her all-white outfit. He shook his head. He reclined in his chair and took a deep swallow of beer. Iris began to settle herself.

Trevor studied her face. She felt the intensity of his attention and looked into his eyes. She gave him a half smile. Then she felt him move toward her.

Slowly, without shifting his gaze, he reached for the mask. He gently pulled it down over her eyes. He smiled.

He leaned into her then, and kissed her. Her mouth parted, and she barely felt his tongue. She had only the smallest taste of him.

He drew back, but only a few inches. For a second she thought he may kiss her again.

Trevor broke into a wide grin. "Let her think about that, Kemosabe."

He settled back into his chair and reached for his beer. Iris let out a small, unanchored laugh. She looked toward the bar, scanning the line for Red Riding Hood. Iris couldn't help it. She had to look.

[Stick Game] Bingo! You won big-time at the tribal casino. Collect $5,000 from the bank. A photograph of you holding your giant check appears in the tribal paper, so everyone knows you have money. Distribute $6,000 to the other players at the table.

[Stick Game] Congratulations! Your three-on-three basketball team won the regional tourney. Collect $500 from the bank and give everyone at the table $20 to celebrate.

[Stick Game] You have just graduated from dental school and taken a job with the IHS. Congratulations! Collect a Pendleton Blanket card from each player.

[Stick Game] Arrows from behind: the Tribal Museum Director has been stealing cornhusk bags and selling them on the internet. She was appointed by the previous Tribal Chair, her husband's cousin, so give $500 to the Tribal Chair at the table and hope he'll press charges.

Trevor convinced Iris that if she were serious about snagging an Indian man, she needed to fish in deeper water. So in mid-November she fired up the Corolla and headed down I-5 for the annual American Indian Film Festival.

Three days later, Iris left San Francisco just after midnight and headed home. She couldn't wait to talk to Trevor, so once she cleared the mountains she pulled into a rest stop and got out her phone. It was six thirty on a Sunday morning. Trevor gave a groggy hello when she called.

"Hey, Trevor, I met somebody."

"Yeah? At the film festival?"

"Yeah, and we made out during this documentary on defor-estation. I felt kind of bad, but the movie was so depressing! You know how that kind of thing just makes you want to escape?"

"Um, no."

"Okay, well, that's what happened."

She heard him change positions, perhaps roll from his back to his stomach. "How very life-affirming of you," he offered.

"Exactly!"

"So where is this guy from?"

"That's the best thing: he's from Kamiah! And he's great. He works for the tribe on salmon restoration."

"Salmon restoration! I like a fish man."

Iris could tell that Trevor was now sitting up.

"I know! He's so amazing. He went to Dartmouth, and then he did a master's in biology at Idaho so he could come back and work for the tribe. He's *totally committed* to our people. He's coming to Portland in a couple of weeks for a conference and he asked me out."

"On a date?"

"Duh! We're having dinner."

"Sounds like it might be more than just a snag."

"Maybe." She drew in a quick breath. "I hope."

"Wait a minute," Trevor said, his voice fully awake. "He does salmon restoration and he was making out during a film on deforestation? Shouldn't he be all worried about that? About riparian zones and shit like that? Who did you say this guy is?"

"Carson," she said. "Carson Lawyer."

There was a long silence at the other end of the line.

Then: "Carson? And he works for the tribe? Kind of a big guy?"

"Yeah. You know him?"

"Yeah, I know Carson," Trevor said. "My sister is having a baby with him."

There was another long pause.

Finally Iris spoke.

"I don't know which one of us should be more pissed off right now," she said. After another pause, she said, "I'm sorry."

"Me, too," he said, and hung up.

TRUST PIT. On the center of the board is an area marked TRUST PIT. The TRUST PIT is the repository for funds taken by the Federal Government. There are three cards marked Trust Pit in the deck of Stick Game cards. If a player draws one of these cards, the player must immediately place all cash assets in the TRUST PIT. All future cash exchanges (gained in Give Aways and passages Home) must be deposited into the TRUST PIT. The player whose assets are taken into trust must simply watch his or her money accumulate throughout the game, as there is no mechanism for removing the funds from trust. If all three Trust Pit cards are drawn by players in the course of one game, the game is immediately over.

Iris was beading the edge of her *wIndin!* game board when Trevor came by, dripping wet from the winter rains. She gave him a cup of hot tea as he settled into the padded folding chair at her table.

"I had an idea for the Stick Game cards today," she said.

"Yeah?"

"It's a special card called Quantum Leap."

"Oh god."

"Awesome, right? So you get the Quantum Leap card, and it says, 'Congratulations! Your auntie got pissed at your mom and told the Enrollment Office that your dad is really not your dad but your mom's old high-school boyfriend. Since he's a full-blood, you

are now 25 percent *more* Indian! Give everyone at the table $20 to celebrate your Quantum Leap!' "

"Okay, but isn't 'high-school boyfriend' kind of tame? How about 'your auntie blabbed that your dad is really some Tohono O'odham dude your mom snagged at Gathering of Nations.' Then you could actually *collect* $20 from everyone at the table so you can make an epic journey back to your roots to find your full-blooded dad."

"And his entire clan. Good luck with that."

"You know, they're all full-bloods down there. They all run around like, 'I'm four/four! I'm four/four!'"

"Be careful, you might end up at law school down there," she said. "How about, 'Your mom just told you that you aren't really her kid but your Aunt Holly's, and your dad is some Quechua guy she met at an anti-Columbus rally.' It would be like, 'Congratulations! You are *really* Indigenous!' "

"You are *transfreakinghemispherically* Indigenous. And you're related to Benjamin Bratt."

"Dang! That's no good. That could *kill* fantasy lives. Should I make the guy Aymaran?"

"Listen, Iris, there's something I've got to talk to you about."

"Does it involve Benjamin Bratt?"

"No."

"Then I'm not sure I'm interested."

"Come *on*, Iris."

"Okay. What." Iris stopped beading and looked up at him.

"I think it's really cool that you are getting your art out there. But I think you should talk to some other artists, you know, get some advice. Maybe help you decide if you should go back to school or figure out the next thing. Because there is more out there than Indian Art Northwest. And Design Depot."

Iris returned to her work. "I think I'll see some artists at the show."

"You mean some *other* artists."

Iris stopped beading and looked up at him. "Look, just because I don't have my life all mapped out like you do doesn't mean that I don't have a plan."

"I know," he said, dropping his gaze. She leaned farther into her work so that Trevor was looking at the top of her head. With her needle, she plucked each bead and drew it into place. The loop of thread tightened and slackened, tightened and slackened.

Suddenly she stopped and looked up at him. "What?" she demanded.

"Nothing." He sat up straighter in his chair.

"I think there's something."

"Okay," he said. "I have something for you." He produced a small white card from his pocket. She laid down her needle and took it from his hand. She recognized the 505 area code, but not the rest of the number. "It's Marcus Amerman's cell," he said, proudly. She stared at the card. "So you can call him," he added.

"And why would I call him?"

"Just to find out if he's coming to Portland in May. And then you can ask to see him."

She laid the card on the table, on the other side of the board. She picked up her needle.

"Look, you call him up and you say, 'You're an artist and I'm an artist and we're both showing at Indian Art Northwest, and I'd like to talk with you.'"

"Right," Iris said, popping a pair of deep blue beads onto her needle. "Then he hangs up on me."

"I don't think he's like that. I think he's chill," Trevor said. "But what if he did—what if he said no?"

Iris didn't speak. She continued to work. Presently she said, "How did you get this?"

Trevor shrugged. "My auntie knows him."

[Stick Game] Your uncle just died and all his kids showed up at the funeral, so now you finally know how many relations you have. Congratulations! Your family has made a Quantum Leap. Give everyone at the table $20 to celebrate.

[Stick Game] Your Tribal Council has voted to extinguish the blood quantum requirement, making tribal membership based on descent and adoption. Congratulations! Your people have made a Quantum Leap. Give each player a horse and burn your CIB card to celebrate.

[Stick Game] Your Tribal Council has voted to exercise its sovereignty by conducting same-sex marriages. Congratulations! Your Council has made a Quantum Leap. All players toss $200 in the TRUST PIT for your Legal Defense Fund.

It was springtime again and forsythia bloomed its brilliant yellow and purple crocus popped out of dark earth. Trevor received acceptance letters from six law schools, including New Mexico, Arizona, Colorado, Washington, Lewis & Clark, and Stanford. Iris was putting the finishing touches on *wIndin!* and beginning work on her next installation piece: a Columbus Day booth for selling absolutions. She planned to set it up next to the

annual Native American Student Association Bake Sale at the university.

Trevor had until April 15 to make his decision about law school, so he and Iris had mapped out a two-week road trip through the West to visit potential institutions. But four days before they were to leave, Iris got a call from home. It was ten thirty at night, and her sister was crying and barely able to speak. Iris understood her well enough: they were all at the hospital, and the priest was on his way.

Iris dialed and held her breath until Trevor answered. She said that she had to go home, that she was leaving right then.

"Come get me," Trevor said. "I'll drive you. I'll take the bus back."

She agreed. She would throw her things in a bag and be right over.

"Iris," he said. "I'm at Brian's."

USUAL AND ACCUSTOMED PLACES. A player who lands on this space should collect five hundred dollars from the bank for each player at the table, then distribute the money equally around the table, much like the Salmon Chief apportions salmon. The ability to apportion correctly is a requirement of the Salmon Chief. The player rolls again.

Trevor opened the door and held his arms wide when Iris arrived. She folded easily into his body. She could hear Brian working in the kitchen, assembling a bag of food for their trip. Brian shortly came out to greet her, handing the bag of sandwiches to Trevor, and telling Iris how sorry he was to hear the

news. His eyes were languid and kind. Trevor stuck his toothbrush in an inside pocket of his bomber jacket and gave Brian a sturdy hug, no kiss.

Trevor and Iris got into the car without speaking. They stopped in Coburg for gas, then Trevor eased back onto I-5. The car sliced dutifully through veils of rain as Iris gazed out the window at the red and gold lights on the back of semis and the regular announcement of towns on road signs that emerged out of the dark with reflective white letters. It went like this for some time, neither of them speaking. Sweet Home. Brownsville. Albany.

Salem. Brooks.

Woodburn. Wilsonville.

Portland.

Troutdale. Hood River.

In The Dalles they stopped at a drive-through for coffee.

At Celilo they stopped to switch drivers. Trevor pulled over and shut down the engine. Iris looked at him wearily.

"Sandwich?" he asked, lifting an offering from the bag.

She nodded. He watched her unwrap the wax paper and take a bite. She felt his attention, and her eyes flashed to meet his. "It's good," she said. He relaxed a little bit. He reached over and laid his hand on the angel wing of her shoulder.

"I don't feel anything," she said.

"That's good," he answered. "That's your body taking care of you, making sure you get home okay. You will feel it when you get there."

They sat together for a while. She gradually felt aware of the weight of his hand on her back.

"How long have you been back with Brian?" she asked.

"Since November. Since . . . Halloween," he said.

"Why didn't you tell me?"

Trevor didn't answer right away. "I don't know. I guess I thought you wouldn't understand. Or that you'd be pissed."

Maybe on another day. Maybe she would have been angry, would have said something. Not today. She leaned back against the seat and Trevor withdrew his hand. She closed her eyes and allowed her head to fall against the headrest. It was quiet except for the gentle cadence of rain hitting the roof.

"My auntie used to talk about this place," she said. "Celilo. She used to come here when she was little."

The rain tapped a muted rhythm on the roof.

"Wyam. That's what my grandmas called it," Trevor said. "*Wyam.*"

"Your family came here, too?"

"Everyone used to come here. And they were here, you know, at the end. On that last day. That last day before they blew it up for the dam." Trevor turned away and peered into the darkness. The sound of cars splitting through water on the freeway surged and faded beyond them. "That last day," Trevor said. "Was your family here? Your auntie?"

"Yeah," she answered, her voice disappearing like vapor.

Tears rose and breached, spilled out of her closed eyes in streams down the sides of her face. She cried absolutely noiselessly. Her body had not yet broken open, but she felt her proximity to that deep river of grief. She no longer felt numb, but rather she felt the accruing weight of loss. She felt that her body was filling with sand.

Trevor stroked her hair, held her hands. After a time, with the chill of the spring rains seeping into the car, she composed herself. Trevor suggested that he continue to drive, and she said yes.

Soon they were traveling through the starry cocoon of a clear night along the Columbia. As they propelled eastward into the

morning sky, the carmine glow of sunrise saturated the car. Just after 5:00 a.m., they crested the final hill to at last see Pendleton laid out before them, twinkling with lights and the early awakenings of dawn. Trevor drove Iris straight to St. Anthony Hospital, but they had already taken the body away.

Trevor merged gracefully into the chaos of a grieving family. There was tremendous work that needed to be done, and he readily made himself useful, as there were people to feed, drummers to assemble, items to be removed from the home of the deceased. Indian people flooded in from every direction, even some of Trevor's relations from Yakama. He slept for short hours on the corners of couches and the back of vans. He barely saw Iris during those blurry and intense days.

After ceremonies that lasted thirty-seven hours straight, Trevor arranged a ride to Portland with one of his cousins. Iris walked him out to the car in the Longhouse parking lot. Her face was swollen and her eyes red from crying, yet she exuded a tranquil sense of self-possession. She embraced him and thanked him. She said that she was sorry to give up her road trip with him, but perhaps he could go with Brian? Trevor said he would give it some thought. He hugged her again, kissed her cheek, then got in the car.

Iris spent four more days at home with her family. On the fifth day, she packed her car and drove back to her apartment. It felt good to drive again. She felt strong. It was springtime.

As she climbed the stairs to her apartment, she saw that an envelope was taped to the door. Iris peeled off the envelope and opened it. As she extracted the letter, a card fell out and fluttered to the floor. She glanced at it, then turned to the letter.

> *Hey Iris,*
>   *We are off to find the most scenic locale for me to get my*

*ass kicked, Socratic-style. I will call you from random places
so PICK UP!*

*I hope that your time at home was everything you needed
it to be.*

The enclosed is for you. You can thank me later.

Love,

T

She carefully folded the letter and placed it back in the enve-
lope. She looked at the card on the floor. She squatted down and
picked it up, stared at its backside for a long, still moment. Then
she turned it over.

Rootless

The problem was, we were trying to board the bus during shift change. We waited as the arriving passengers streamed out, but the second my foot touched the step, the bus driver's hand went up. "You gotta wait, Miss." She pointed to a cordoned-off area on the sidewalk approximately five feet away. "You wait over there."

A burly man and I exchanged looks, then wheeled our bags the long way around to reassemble behind the flat yellow tape. Perhaps it was the heat, or perhaps it was to cover our docility, but we did nothing to intercept the thin woman. We just stood there and watched her attempt to board the bus, observing the driver's mouth move and the finger point in our direction.

The woman maneuvered into line with us. She wore jeans and a linen tunic, and her longish blond hair in bangs. The man stepped back and gestured for her to get in line in front of him. The new driver, carrying a small bag and clipboard, arrived and boarded the bus.

"The air is thick here," the woman said. "Is the air thick here?"

I scanned the bunch grass of the estuary, then the sky above the city. "Yes," I said, although I had no real basis for my statement.

The doors of the bus snapped open and the first driver stepped out, waving goodbye to the new one.

"I haven't been here for two years," the woman said. "Lost a lot of weight since then. Seventy pounds."

"Really?" I asked, and saw the burly man turn his face toward us. The woman looked like the type who had been thin all her life, and seventy extra pounds was something to picture. "How did you do it?"

"Stress."

The bus woke with a rumble and rolled forward five feet, exhaling as it stopped in front of us. The doors popped open and we boarded. The woman slid into the row of seats that faced the baggage rack, and I sat down, too, not too close. Her hair was flecked with gray, and her forearms were covered with freckles.

"I've been taking photographs for the last nine years. In *Nevada*. Virginia City," she said. "Taking photographs of *tourists*! Can you believe it? People come from all over the world to dress up like cowboys and whores."

The woman carried a soft brown leather purse, the kind sewn with the nap side out, with a long shoulder strap. It was trimmed with turquoise beads and fringe. She held a thick paperback novel called *Shenandoah* on her lap.

"You don't have any bags," I said, as the bus pulled away from the curb.

"That's right." She threw her hands in the air. "It's an adventure!"

Just then my phone rang. I fished it out from my bag, pushing aside a small container of camas roots. I was returning home from Root Feast on the Rez, or maybe I was returning to exile, taking my roots with me. It doesn't seem right that one should be returning on both ends of a journey, but that's how it felt. On the phone I explained to my boyfriend that my plane had been delayed, so

I would be at the station a bit later. "Call me when you get to MacArthur," he said.

When I hung up, the woman said, "If you ever run away from home, hold on to that thing. Because you just can't put a coin in a box anymore."

"No, I guess not."

"You can't even *find* a pay phone. When did that happen?"

"It's too bad. Sometimes you need a phone like that."

She shrugged. "What are you going to do?"

The bus rolled noisily past warehouses and taco trucks. She leaned toward me. "Will you help me listen? For the station? I have trouble," she said, pointing to her right ear.

"Oh," I said. "Don't worry. The shuttle goes straight there. No stops."

"And which one?"

"Coliseum."

"Is it south or north of the city?"

"South."

"Okay. I'm going to Albany."

"That's bit north."

"Yeah, my friend is going to meet me."

"There's no stop in Albany."

"Okay. Then the next stop?"

"El Cerrito."

"El Cerrito stop. Thank you for being so kind."

I told her it was nothing. It is no hardship to recite the train schedule.

"We're going to the ocean, going to get some air. You know there is less oxygen in Nevada? Sixteen percent less oxygen at that elevation."

"Wow."

"I'm glad to be out of there."

"I bet."

"This morning I left my cat and my husband."

"For good? Or just—temporarily?"

"For good. Yeah."

I didn't say anything. I felt bad about the cat. I've left men before. I wondered if I should say something about the cat. Neither of us said anything for a few minutes, and then I realized that she was crying.

"That crazy bastard damn near broke my nose," she said. A laugh sputtered out. "Now I don't know what."

"You're doing the right thing."

"Tell me I can't cry here," she said. "I can cry when I get to my friend's house. But not here. Can't be crying in Oakland."

People cry in Oakland. But I knew what she meant.

"That's right," I said. "Stiff upper lip, then."

I felt awkward saying it, but I felt a moral obligation to be chipper.

She wiped her eyes quickly with an index finger. "I'll just cry into my hat," she said. She choked on a laugh again. "But I forgot my hat."

"Now *there's* the tragedy."

She nodded and choked some more. "You're good," she said. "That *is* a tragedy. You can't go outside without a hat in Nevada."

"No. That sun will kill you."

"I can't believe I left it."

I wanted to say that she would get a new hat, but I didn't want to burden her with metaphors. The bus arrived at the station and we filed out. The woman went to buy a ticket, and I took the stairs to the platform.

Falling Crows

The boy who is coming home with part of himself missing is the man's nephew. The man, Silas, receives the news and hangs up the phone, numb. He wants a drink. He doesn't want a drink. He wants time to move backward.

Silas is attempting to become a better sort of man, the kind who allows his feelings to muscle their way to the surface like a crocus. This is what Silas wants. But when he considers his emotional life he sees a bed of angry flowers. Better to keep those underground. His inner life is van Gogh in Saint-Rémy, not Arles. He thinks about his nephew, the littlest one, and he feels a blankness rimmed with fury.

Water. He hears himself say the word, and his legs carry him to the sink. His eyes watch distant arms operate the smooth coordination of faucet and glass. Action and reaction. Physics. Life was a series of entirely predictable events.

And yet.

The boy would be flown to Portland. He would have reconstructive surgery and rehab. He would walk again.

Silas puts down the glass. He thinks about his sister; he thinks about his nephew, who is not a boy but a man; he thinks about the magpie outside, hopping off a low branch into the grass. He tries to imagine his nephew without a foot, a hand, a cheek. It is

hard to do. Joseph had been a beautiful boy with smooth skin and a muscular, pulsing body. To think of him draped in white sheets and swathed in bloody gauze, taped to a hospital bed and only moving the fingers of his remaining hand, was to imagine another person entirely. Silas imagines Joseph's fingers crawling after the morphine button. Silas shakes his head to dismiss the picture, even as he feels his own hand clench.

On the same day that Silas hears that his nephew is coming home, he gets a phone call from the Tribal Office. A courier has brought a package. Can he come?

The boy who is coming home without his leg, arm, and cheek is the woman's son. The woman, Joanna, is not afraid to see him in his wounded state; she is his mother and wants only to hold him, to feel him breathe, to hear his voice. He is alive, and he has more life ahead. He is a man; he is her boy.

She is driving to Portland. She prays as she drives. She prays the humble, mercy-begging prayers of a mother who has been saved from the abyss; hers are the prayers of a person just re-deemed. The grief will come later, in some ordinary moment: standing in line at the grocery store, folding the laundry, washing the spoon that she has just used to feed her grown son.

Some time after the shock, some time after the grief, and without her knowing why, she will blame herself. This too will be a sudden confession, banal and absurd, like a can of store biscuits popping open in the heat. *Koof!* She will hear herself talking then, and not understand; she will say: *My son nearly died and it was my fault.*

Joanna is alone in the car because she could not wait for anyone.

She could have walked across the road to talk to Silas but she didn't have the time. There was no time! Instead she called him on the phone, asked him to look after her dog and horses. Then she ran out of the house without locking the doors.

Joanna keeps her eyes on the road, her hands fixed at ten and two, though she recently heard that nine and three were just as good, or even better for modern cars. She doesn't change the dial on the radio even as the banter between the DJs turns increasingly inane. She does not care about the latest Kanye meme, or what happened to the DJ while she was at the DMV, or about that new app that makes things appear and then disappear. She does not want free concert tickets; she does not want to be the tenth caller. Joanna knows that soon she will drive into range of KWSO from Warm Springs, and she will know she is almost to Portland. She doesn't touch the dial; she doesn't waste gestures. She doesn't want to slow down. She wants time to jump ahead.

She thinks about the day Joseph came home from school and told her what he wanted to do, that he wanted to enlist. She did not stop him. Like her own mother, Joanna wanted her children to fly away like meadowlarks, free. Joanna thinks about her mother. She thinks about a small replica of Michelangelo's *Pietà*, placed on the mantle in her childhood home. It was almost too beautiful to look at: the still-young Mary holding her broken son, sprawled in death across her lap. Joanna thinks about Mary's placid expression. Mary's calm face, Joanna had been taught, was the model of pious acceptance. *No*, Joanna thinks. It could not be acceptance. *It is shock*; this is what Joanna knows now. Why did Joanna stare at the statue so often? Was it the pathos? Or was it the form? Mary's

body rises up, solid. She is a pyramid, ancient and unmovable. The perfect mountain that is Mary holding Jesus illustrates a basic fact of science: the triangle is the most sturdy structure in all of nature.

Joanna pictures herself as Mary, imagines Joseph in his man's body on her lap, limp and beyond the world of cares. When he was small, Joseph would fall asleep that way, with utter unconcern, even after he became too big for her lap. He would sleep through church and council meetings and even basketball games like that. Joseph was her youngest, the *laymíwt*, and Joanna held on to him as long as she could.

She wonders if she held on to him too much. If that led to this.

Joanna follows the road as it turns to run alongside the Columbia. She calms in the companionship of the river, though she keeps the pressure steady on the gas.

She is Mary; she is the sturdiest structure in nature.

She is not Mary; she is not.

A courier is waiting for Silas. He listens to the message a second time and decides to drive to the office. He claps the pickup door closed and contemplates his bare hands for a moment. Is it worth walking back to the house for his gloves? Winter is approaching, announcing its intent with bitter wind. Silas cups his hands around his mouth and blows. His breath rolls off the rough surface. No, he decides, and leans in to start the engine.

Silas has tattoos on his knuckles, his hands. Not the pretty kind. He has other ones too, fancy designs that climb up his arms, his chest, his back. He drives to the tribal admin building and parks. On his way to his office he stops to visit Wilda, a woman who has seen all of his tattoos and most of his scars.

He leans on the doorframe of her office. She looks up but doesn't smile. This is her friendly face.

"Council's declaring a State of Emergency," she says.

Silas does not know what to say because he doesn't know which emergency is now an Emergency. Forest fires? Schools? Roads? Diabetes? *What to say.* Silas is caught between his desire to be a better man and his desire not to implicate himself in Not Listening. He decides to thread the needle.

"You think it will make a difference?" he asks.

"Maybe," she says. "If it's not just talk." She takes a sip of tea from her KEEP CALM AND POWWOW ON mug.

Silas nods. Wilda hates any form of linguistic anemia. Wilda knows that words are imbued with power; she was born to be a lawyer. Nothing annoys her more than empty declarations, whether in politics or advertising or love. She would not congratulate the council for putting a name to a problem that everyone could see on its face. No revelations there; no discoveries in that. To declare a State of Emergency was to pull a fire alarm. Either people would get up and run, or not.

Silas clears his throat.

He tells Wilda that Joseph is coming home, and Joanna has gone to meet him. He says it evenly, conscious of how the news will sound to her. He knows that Wilda has made that drive herself, when her daughter, Chloe, was in a car crash with her high-school friends. Chloe survived for several days in the hospital before she passed. Then Wilda became the survivor.

Silas does not want his words to wound her, to send her back in time.

"Oh," Wilda says. "That's good he's coming home." She tells Silas that she will pray for them. He thanks her. Everyone on the reservation prays, either to God or Creator or both. Silas does

not consider himself a devotional man. Yet he speaks in sweats and the Longhouse, and never fails to assume proper posture at public ceremonies: hand on heart, turn to the left, release hand to sky. The body makes its own prayer, even without words. Sometimes Silas imagines the light map of North America at night, but instead of showing the concentration of light around the cities, it radiates the steady blink of Indian prayers. That's a new map: a map of small, bleating clusters around Oakland, Denver, and Chicago, and luminous swaths at Umatilla, Lapwai, Colville, Lame Deer, Standing Rock, Winnipeg, Yellowknife, Lawrence, Window Rock.

Wilda suggests that Silas come over for dinner.

He takes in her words. Wilda is staring up at him, and after a moment he realizes that he is standing in the door for too long, as though he were actually attached to the doorframe, as though he were himself a door ajar. He dislodges himself and steps back. He says he needs to get to the office and that there's a package waiting for him. He says he will come for dinner and thanks her.

"You can thank Earl," she says. "He's the one who got the deer."

Earl, Silas thinks as he walks away. *Yes, he's the one.*

The one who is in the hospital bed without a shin, a wrist, or an earlobe is the young woman's brother. The young woman, Joy, happens to be crying when she gets the news, but the shock makes her stop. For a moment her heartbreak recedes, a wide river dammed. She walks to the living room to sit down on a chair that is no longer there. She goes to the kitchen to make tea, but the kettle is gone. Joy wonders where she can go where she will not see that something is not there. In her home she is surrounded by

unmatched pairs: the sofa without the chair, the cup without the kettle, the air without the love. In the kitchen, Joy puts her hand on her heart and prays. As she finishes she turns around and lifts her hand to the sky, a gesture that is part request and part sigh, and part wish that M. would come back.

M. is not coming back. Joy knows this. But Joy has a stubborn heart.

Joy's name is aspirational, which is not to say that she lacks optimism. Joy believes in love; even after M. leaves, Joy does not regret her love. She wants more love, more love. She listens to the black-capped chickadees chattering in the bushes outside. This is the only love she feels now. She wants to fill herself with the sound. Joy tries to find love in everything: the birds, the trees, the rumble of trucks in the street. She believes that love is everywhere, and aches that love is so diffuse she cannot hold on to it. Love is an ax in her chest and a bird in flight. But Joy believes love will not always leave; someday it will stay. Joy may be the Most Optimistic Person in North America. Her parents should have named her Hope.

Joy is relieved that her little brother is coming home. She is the middle child of three, the peacemaker. Their older sister, Naomi, is a nurse in Toronto with a husband and two children. Joy wonders when Naomi will come, if she will come. Joy does not know the extent of Joseph's injuries, so she imagines him whole, just as he was before he left. She knows she must go to the hospital, and starts to prepare: brush teeth, shoe feet, jacket body, hat head. Each little task gives her some relief, some sense of purpose. There is comfort in the reliable needs of a crisis. She steps outside and turns to lock the door. Gray clouds, weary of carrying rain, unburden themselves as she walks to the bus stop. She breathes deep the cold, moist air. She feels good to be outside,

glad to interrupt the endless wandering around the house. At the bus stop, waiting, she wonders if she is a bad person for feeling relief that one emergency is displacing the pain of another. She feels slightly guilty about this, but tells herself it isn't math. It's life. Waiting for the bus she digs her hands deeper into her pockets, and contemplates the PSA poster fixed to the shelter wall: DIRECT PRESSURE STOPS BLEEDING.

At the office, Silas approaches his cubicle and sees the courier sitting in the chair beside the desk. The courier is a young man in a turquoise Patagonia jacket, holding a box in his lap. Tufts of brown curls poke out from under his dark blue knit cap. He stands when he sees Silas approach the cubicle, cradling the box in one arm.

"Osiyo, Mr. Shield," he says, extending his hand.

Silas smiles, shakes the man's hand. "'Siyo," Silas says. "That's one of only two Tsalagi words I know. Half my vocabulary right there."

"But 'siyo and Tsalagi are two words."

"Ah," Silas says. "It's two-thirds then."

The man introduces himself as Adam Sixkiller, and they sit down. Adam continues to hug the box as he explains that he is delivering a package that he was afraid to mail for fear it might be lost or damaged. Adam is a graduate student in linguistics, and had been hired to clean out the office of a professor who had unexpectedly passed away. The professor had studied phonology of several West African languages.

Adam opens the box and shows Silas the contents: a dozen reel-to-reel tapes. The top box is labeled NEZ PERCE. JANUARY 10, 1957.

"These are not his recordings," Adam says. "I don't think anyone knows that he had them. I want to give them back to the tribe."

Silas studies the contents for a moment.

"Nobody knows that *I* have them," Adam adds.

"You want to take them to the Language Program then?" Silas asks. "This is Natural Resources here."

"I could do that," Adam says. "But I wanted to talk to you first." He reaches in the box and extracts a tape. He flips it over to show Silas the back: FLORA MEDICINE SHIELD AND BESSIE MONTIETH. "These are your relations?"

Silas nods.

"They made all of these tapes. I don't know how they ended up in that office. There's no record of the person who made them, besides these two speakers. There's a man's voice on the tape but no ID, and I don't think any linguist would do that. They could be homemade tapes that someone found in an attic or closet and gave to the university. Gave them to the only linguist they knew, I would guess, because otherwise it really doesn't make sense."

Nothing makes sense, Silas thinks. *Making sense is an unhealthy attachment.*

"Do you want to take them?" Adam asks. "These are the originals, and I did not make copies."

"No copies at the university?"

"Not that I could find."

"Seems like a strange thing for a linguist to do. To not make a copy."

Adam stiffens: shoulders back, chin forward.

"Mr. Shield, I'm a citizen of the Cherokee Nation before I am a linguist."

Silas nods. He finds Adam's patriotism endearing. *That's just*

how the Cherokees talk, he thinks to himself. To Adam he says, "All right then."

Adam passes the box to Silas, and he takes it. For a moment Silas feels a flash of pain and perhaps fear; this is the anxiety that blooms from inheriting a dying language. *No, not dying*, he thinks, *only endangered*. To be in danger is to be in a state of perpetual vigilance; it is fight or flight every day. Silas knows this. He feels the magnitude of treasure in his arms, and the intense pressure of keeping it safe. *Fight or flight*. A wave of failure washes over him. He straightens his back. He nestles the box in the curve of his left arm, and extends his right hand to Adam.

"Wado," he says.

It's Song Dedication Hour on KWSO when Joanna reaches the signal.

This one is going out from Ted to Doris: "Always on My Mind" by Willie Nelson. And good luck, Ted! Joanna listens to the lyrics and feels relieved to think about someone else's story. *What did you do, Ted?* she wonders. *What did you not do, Ted?* If Will were here, she thinks, they would be making up a story and how things went horribly wrong with Doris and Ted. Song dedication shows had been their companion through many long road trips, especially late at night. Along those dark highways, their children sleeping on each other's shoulders in the back seat, they would string stories like beads into elaborate patterns, usually to make each other laugh. Will could always make her laugh, and the Song Dedication game was one of their favorites. Sometimes, though, they would get stumped. Sometimes songs were too sad, and they had to admit there was nothing their imagined Ted could do that would redeem him for taking Doris for granted all those years.

All right, our next caller is Lisa in Madras. She's thinking about Dave tonight, and this one travels the airwaves straight to his heart: Mariah Carey's "We Belong Together." Hope you're paying attention, Dave! Joanna smiles at the DJ's commentary. There are so few of these shows anymore. How do people manage without them? So unfortunate that yearning lovers are reduced to sharing their actual feelings without the persuasive ventriloquism of R&B or country or even grunge. This is another strike against the modern age.

And here's a real good one, all acoustic. From Aaron to Sandra, here's "Wildflowers" by Tom Petty. Joanna draws a quick breath, and for a moment she cannot move. She hasn't heard this song since Jim Boyd came down from Colville to sing it at Will's funeral. That was Will's request, to have her famous, gifted cousin sing at his farewell. *You belong among the wildflowers / You belong on a boat out at sea . . .*

And now Jim is gone too.

Sail away, kill off the hours / You belong somewhere you feel free . . .

Joanna's hand jumps off the wheel to turn off the radio. She feels it has wounded her, cut through her when she was not expecting it. She remembers what her grandmother told her, that there was no Nez Perce word for radio. That is, there was no one word for radio. Every family made up their own word, and this revealed a lot about what people thought of it. Some people made words that meant "the thing that talks all the time" or "the thing that gossips" or "the thing that sings." Joanna fixes her eyes on Mount Hood and drives steadily toward it, only her breath as company now.

What is the radio to her? A voice without a body. A force without form.

The thing that woos.

The thing that wounds.

The thing that remembers.

—

The sliding glass doors admit Joy to the lobby and instantly her body recalls times past, when her family spent days and nights with Will in the oncology ward, praying for a recovery that never came. Not at this hospital, but no matter. To her, all hospitals smell the same: clean and anxious.

She heads to the fourth floor. She nods at the nurses when they look up from their station. Joy feels a pang in her chest, wishing Naomi were with her now. Passing the station, Joy feels she is trespassing on a secret social world that only the nurses share; the hospital is their own little city. Joy finds Joseph's room and stops at the door, her heart pounding. She looks in and sees him sleeping; she sees the bandages on his face and the tubes snaking up his arm. She takes in the shape of his body under the sheets, the stumps of arm and leg on his left side. She thinks she might vomit.

She steps back and breathes.

She goes in, walks straight to his side. She fixes her eyes on his face. She wants to wrap her arms around him but has no idea how. So many tubes and wires! She wedges herself between the bed and a monitor and gently places her palm on the top of his head. He stirs and turns his head.

"Joseph," she says, and he opens his eyes.

The sound of monitors is not the song of birds.

The scent of disinfectant is not the aroma of skin.

The blood of strangers delivered by gravity and a needle is not the blood that runs through your mother's heart when she carried you.

Joanna arrives at the door and pauses. She sees Joseph

sleeping; she sees Joy rise from the chair beside his bed. She sees nobs of blanketed flesh where once were muscular limbs.

It seems that time has stopped, but Joanna knows that it is only she who has stopped. She is so close to him now, and for one moment she feels the chasm: he on one side, and she on the other. A mother is the vanguard of her children, but Joseph went out ahead. She sees that he has been changed, and yet he is still exactly himself. At once she makes her way, reaching with both hands to him, eager now as the day he was born to draw him to herself.

On the way home from Wilda and Earl's house, Silas is singing to himself. He gradually becomes aware of the tune: "Waiting in Vain" by Bob Marley. He ponders the significance of this. He notices, for the first time, that *girl* rhymes with *Earl*. Silas smiles. A little joke that he will keep to himself.

If summer is here, I'm still waiting there / Winter is here, and I'm still waiting there . . .

Is this what all heartbreak comes down to? Silas wonders. *Timing?*

Silas sings to himself, and thinks about the venison stew that Wilda made with the deer that Earl brought home. *I don't wanna wait in vain for your love . . .* If there were a Song Dedication Hour on the local station, Silas would send this one out. But there isn't. And he can't.

It's painful for Joseph to talk at first.

The first thing he says is: "I never liked M."

"What?" Joy asks. "Are you serious?"

Joseph half smiles. "No. I just said that to make you feel better." He licks his lips. His throat is dry. He looks up at Joy. "I always liked M. I'm sorry you broke up."

Joy does not know how to accept her brother's comfort. "Thanks?" she says.

"You're going to be okay," he says.

"You, too," she says, and squeezes his hand.

"Ouch!"

"Sorry!"

"Just kidding. That's my good hand. I mean, that's my hand."

Joy laughs, even though she doesn't want to.

The next time Joseph talks, he's angry. He's angry at his mangled body; he's tormented by his memories of the moment *just before*. He was running, trying to get to cover. Then. Nothing.

Over and over, his penultimate step plays in his mind. The sun pressing down on him. The ground vibrating with explosions. One fluid step, then another. Then.

The silent movie plays the same loop over and over again. Black-and-white. Time stuck in a loop.

He wonders where his leg was lost. On the street? In the hospital? Who was the last person to touch his hand?

He never says *why me?* He just says: *godDAMNit.*

At home, Silas unloads the tapes on his bedside shelf. They sit in a tidy stack, silent. He has no equipment to play them, so he can only wonder what they hold. He knows that the tapes contain his grandmothers' voices. He hates to admit it, but he's not uncomfortable with this state of suspension. It seems the only way to keep

the past from crashing into the present. A part of him doesn't want to hear them; he doesn't want to hear words he once knew or feel his failure to remember, to speak. At the same time, he aches to hear them again; he remembers how the older ones used to talk, how they laughed and joked. He longs to be at their table again.

The morning of the fifth day Joseph receives two visitors: young men, both Marines in civilian clothes. Buff and healthy. The taller one has a perfect fade, sharp cheekbones, and a prosthetic arm. Joseph wonders when the VA started making prostheses in different flesh tones. The shorter one has blue eyes and a receding hairline. They tell Joseph that they've been exactly where he is now: injured in combat, missing a leg, an arm; feeling alone and angry and scared. Discouraged. Depressed. Hopeless. And guilty that they survived when others didn't.

Whatever you feel is the right way to feel, they say. *You are not alone. Your guys are alive because of what you did.*

Before they leave, the physical therapists arrive.

Time to stand up! they say. This is what it takes to heal. The PTs maneuver Joseph to the edge of the bed. There is an elaborate choreography of shifting tubes and monitors and catheter bag. Joseph winces in pain; he groans; he yelps and curses. Joanna slips her body under Joseph's right arm. The tall marine anchors himself to Joseph on his wounded side, hands on ribs and back.

As Joanna leans into Joseph's side, a clear vision comes to her: Joseph at Grand Entry, with new regalia. She imagines him leading the procession with the other vets. A red bandolier bag with a wide sash across his chest. Floral design. Elaborate cuffs with long fringe. New moccasins, fitted to the prosthesis. And then there would be parades! He would ride, and his Appaloosa would wear

a spectacular martingale and beaded bridle. Joanna's mind races forward; she knows what she must do.

On the count of three they rise.

Joseph's words fall hard between labored breaths.

Now what? he asks.

The next time Joseph talks, he cries. Joanna is alone with him. She doesn't hear him cry; she sees his shoulders shake. He brings his hand to his face, covers his eyes.

"Joseph," she says, coming to his side.

He shakes his head. No, no, no. When he speaks, his voice is high and thin.

"I lost Dad," he says. He cries harder, places his hand on his chest. Eyes squeeze tight and tears roll down the sides of his face.

"No," Joanna says. "No, you can't lose him."

But she knows what he means. She knows that he has, again, lost his father. When Will was diagnosed, he and Joseph got matching tattoos on their left calves, an image to represent Will's Indian name. Who ever thought Joseph would lose his leg? But he did lose it, and he blames himself because that part of Will was something he was meant to have forever. Of course he would feel this way, Joanna thinks. A new loss unstitches the grief that came before. She tries to comfort Joseph but she cannot properly hold him. She gives him her hand to hold, her voice to soothe, but it is not enough.

Joy is moving through her days without fire, without light. Her heartache is replaced with emptiness, and she feels less alive. In the fresh cut of grief, the city had kaleidoscoped with color:

children in orange raincoats and commuters on blue bicycles erupted through the gray slate of rain. The world had been saturated with senseless, brilliant color, but with time a dull buzz like static had set in. She misses that intensity now.

Joanna brings Joy a new kettle. She tells Joy to stop pining over M.

"You can't spend your life wishing for the past," Joanna says. "Look at your little brother. He's not wallowing. He's picking himself up."

Joy resents the comparison. *No one can compete with a man who is trying to walk with one leg*, she thinks.

Then she feels worse.

To her mother she says: *I'm not pining.*

The next time she visits Joseph, she brings a legal pad. Joanna holds it perpendicular to Joseph's leg and he presses his foot against it. Joy makes four attempts to trace his foot but either his foot jerks away or her hand slips.

"Jeez, Joy, just give me the pencil," he says.

"You can't even bend."

"Yeah, and I could still do better than you."

Joy sighs. "Look, do you want this or not?"

Joseph makes a tiny motion with his chin to indicate Joanna, who at that moment is flattening the blanket under his heel. The sudden hush is obvious.

"What?" Joanna asks, looking up.

"I *do* want them," Joseph says.

Nice cover, Joy thinks, and gets it on the fifth try.

At home, as Joy is cutting the pattern, she bursts into tears. *I can't do this*, she says. Joanna slips her arms around her daughter.

"He's not the same," Joy says. "*We're* not the same."

"He has a long road ahead," Joanna says. "And so do you."

She strokes Joy's hair. "But this is what it takes. No matter how you feel, no matter what you are going through, you've got to have your hands on what is good. You've got to be touching the good in life."

The forecast is for a cold winter. It is late afternoon, and Silas puts on his coat to cross the road and feed Joanna's horses. Dark clouds shift above, and a bitter wind charges over the hill. Silas tips his face to the sky and watches two red-winged blackbirds pester and poke at a hawk in flight. *As long as the birds stay in the air, we're good,* Silas thinks. He watches them fly to the north.

In 1788 the winter was so cold that crows froze to death and fell out of the sky midflight. Silas knows this because he studied the Lakota winter counts, saw the image repeated over and over, the crows cast down like ebony hail. He no longer takes it for granted that flying birds will continue on their aerial path. *What did the people think,* he would wonder, *seeing the crows tumble down from the sky, shiny wings flat and twisted like broken kites? Did it seem like the end of the world?*

What was it to see those new terrors? Bright red paint punctuated the winter counts: bodies covered in pustules, a gunshot wound pouring blood, an impudent flag planted on a military fort. Amid these scenes were images of the remarkable, if not the apocalyptic: a year of plenty of buffalo, a year that the river flooded, a year when they stole five Kiowa horses. It was never the end of the world. And it was always the end of the world. Five hundred years into this, and Indian people are still seeing new horrors. Facts of nature that were known and safe—that flying birds would stay in the sky, or that songs would bring people home—suddenly become strange and unreliable.

Silas stops at the mailbox and finds three bills and the tribal paper. As he holds the thin envelope from the utility, he feels pleased that his solar panels were a prudent investment. As an employee of the Natural Resources and Sustainability Division for the tribe, he takes pride in leading by example. When he came back to work for the tribe, he had been asked to work for the Language Program, because as a child he had lived with his grandmother, who only spoke tito·qatímtki at home. He had told them no, he had forgotten everything. To himself he said: *It's buried too far down.* So now he focuses on solar panels and First Foods habitat, which seem, on the whole, fixable.

He opens the electric bill and sees that his solar panels are providing excess energy, so much, in fact, that he is selling energy back to the utility. This development evokes in him mixed feelings: pride in success, yet discomfort at contributing to a corporate energy enterprise.

He unfolds the paper and reads the banner: *Tribal Council Declares State of Emergency over Youth Suicide.*

Silas looks up at the birdless expanse.

What is happening? he says to the sky.

He goes inside and repacks the tapes.

Joanna fills in the background with light blue beads, and Joy is working on the petals of a flower. The PTs have taken Joseph down the hall, so the two are alone in his room.

"I like that spot of green in your pattern there," Joanna says. "It reminds me of Alice." Alice is Joanna's best friend.

"Really?"

"Yeah. It makes me think of her. Because when she was young, she ran off with this Aleut guy that she met at Chemawa. Peter Kashevarof. She always said those schools were good for getting Indians married off to each other."

"I can't picture Alice running off with anyone. She's so religious."

"She was in love! And they didn't run off so much as they got married and went back to his village."

"Mom, that's the opposite of running off."

"Well, she left school to get married, so it was . . . dramatic. Anyway, she was living with his family up there and they had three little children. And then he left her. In a helicopter! Just flew away. Can you imagine?"

"Yes."

"Joy, really? Can you imagine being left on a tiny island in the Bering Strait with three little children and no support except his family, who blames you for his leaving?"

Joy stops beading and considers the question.

"I can't imagine anyone not liking Alice."

"The point is, she was far from everything she had known before, and she had these little children to look after, and her heart was broken. She was so young too. This was the 1970s, and the mail only came once a month on a helicopter, and on that day the whole village would go down to meet it. *That was it* for contact with the outside world! One day she was waiting there, ice and snow everywhere, feeling so low. And as she's scanning the tundra she notices a tiny little spot of green. A little tiny spot of grass peeking through, and she feels some hope. That's what got her through that hard time."

"I think I need more than a patch of grass in the snow."

"I know. We all want more than that. But sometimes that's all you get."

Joseph gets stronger every day, and so does his anger. He says he wants his dreams to stop, but the painkillers force him to sleep. Joanna calls Silas and asks him to come.

Silas is a good uncle, so he makes the drive to Portland. He drops off the tapes at an audio shop to be transferred to digital, and stays with a friend who always has a bed for him when he's in town. He takes Joanna to lunch before she heads back home for a few days. Then he heads to the hospital.

"Lay*míwt!*" he greets his nephew. Joseph smiles at the nickname, even though he's tried to outgrow it all of his life. In the old stories, the laymíwt, the youngest one, is always the hero.

"Hey, Uncle," he says.

"You picked up any eagle feathers yet?"

"Yeah, during surgery. My doctor dropped one. Had to stop everything! Everyone standin' around, waiting for me to come out from anesthesia. You'd think doctors would do better at tying them feathers down."

Silas smiles at the joke. Things seem not so bad. He pulls up the chair and tells Joseph about the tapes.

Joseph tells Silas that Joy has gone back to work and visits in the evenings. Silas asks how she's doing.

"She's better than she thinks she is," Joseph says. "She'll find someone new."

"Probably," Silas says. He gazes out the window at the city,

his view pixelated by the steady transmission of rain on the window.

"What about you?" Silas asks. "Anyone special?"

"Do nurses count?"

"Everything counts."

"Oh, then. No."

They both laugh.

"Someday," Silas says.

"You think someone will look past this?"

"No reason to look past it."

Silas searches his mind for something more to say, but everything he comes up with sounds trite. *It's what's on the inside.* No. *Any woman would be lucky to have you.* No. *You are more than the sum of your parts.* No, no, no. Then he remembers a story.

"There were these two brothers," he says. "They farmed out there, between Umatilla and Pilot Rock. One day there was a problem with the baler; something was stuck in there. And as one brother was trying to repair it, the other brother accidentally hit the lever."

Joseph winces.

"Yeah, it was bad," Silas says. "The one brother lost both arms. He almost bled to death. And then the other brother was really messed up, because he was responsible. And people wondered how the one who was hurt would do—what would happen to him? Would he be able to work? Would his wife still love him? But you know, he survived okay. People took care of him. A few years later, he had another baby, his wife loved him, things were pretty good. It was the other brother who came apart. He started drinking. His wife left him. His life was ruined."

They sit together quietly then.

"What about you, Uncle?"

Silas shakes his head.

Joseph tells Silas that he wants to hear the tapes. He knows that this is what Silas wants, and perhaps why Silas has come. Joseph sees his uncle's wounds.

So one morning Silas brings the recordings to Joseph's bedside. He pushes play and the words roll out from the laptop speaker. Joseph watches as Silas tips his head back, eyes closed, and listens. Silas is still as a monk.

Joseph can't make out the stories, but he recognizes the rhythms of speech, and he catches words here and there. Sometimes he hears a man's voice in the background, or a dog barking. A child speaks, then seems to leave. The women laugh a lot, but sometimes their tone is serious, and sometimes a long pause connects words or thoughts. These silences are dense with feeling. The sounds make Joseph long for a world he barely sensed and never truly knew. He hears screen doors creak open and closed, the low hum of a generator, a radio voice that goes on, then off. Joseph pictures his great-grandmother's house as he knew it from photos: the gingham curtains, a bowl of apricots on the counter, peonies blooming in a vase, a table ringed by wooden chairs. He listens to the mix of their voices and the ambient sounds, and the hospital room is filled with that time, which does not move forward or back, but rests in the lap of the present.

Joseph hears a word he recognizes.

"X̣áx̣a·c," Joseph says. "Grizzly Bear."

Silas stops the recording.

"Yes," Silas says. "They're talking about a man, Fierce Grizzly

Bear. He was attacked by Grizzly Bear, and he fought back. The bear's paw left deep cuts across his chest." Silas drew his hand from his left shoulder to his right hip, fingers curved like claws, to demonstrate. "But the man survived. As he was recovering, intense visions came to him. Grizzly Bear came into the man's dreams and gave him permission to use his wounds as a symbol of his bravery. After that, the man beaded a bandolier with five parallel lines, tapered at both ends, to show Grizzly Bear's claw marks from the fight.

"So my grandmothers, they're telling the story of how this design started to be used. Not just by Fierce Grizzly Bear, but by certain powerful families. It was a sign of respect. They're talking about an old photograph of six Indian scouts, and three of them are wearing bandoliers with this design, five long claw marks across the chest, going left to right."

"I think I know that photo," Joseph says.

"Maybe so. It's in the Council chambers."

"Mom's making a bandolier for me. Woodland design. Like I survived a fight with a florist."

"Hey, that's fierce too!"

Joseph rolls his eyes.

"You know why she's doin' that, don't you?" Silas asks.

"She always does that design."

"She misses your dad, and it reminds her of him. They had that rivalry about where the floral pattern came from—he said we got it from the Ojibwe and she said that they got it from us."

Joseph smiles, remembering. His parents used to tease each other a lot. He thinks of their wedding photo, his father wearing the beaded sash and moccasins that his mother had made. Woodland design.

"She wants things to go back," Joseph says.

"It makes her feel better," Silas says. "To feel like she can do something."

"She can't. No one can do nothing."

"She can't do nothing."

"Right."

"I'm not agreeing with you, son. I'm telling you: she *can't do* nothing."

Joseph sighed.

"Maybe a design will come to you and you can tell her."

"My dreams aren't like that."

"Doesn't have to be a dream," Silas says. "Could be some other way."

After a moment, Silas gets a notebook and pen from his bag and restarts the recording. Joseph thinks about his mother and the flowers blooming under her fingertips. He thinks of her pulling each thread, drawing snug each bead to hide, one by one. He watches Silas write words and fragments.

Joseph closes his eyes, perhaps to sleep. The sound of the old language flows around him; he feels he is floating, or riding a great river. When he sleeps he can forget what he has lost, but then he wakes to his mismatched limbs and he remembers. This is what life is now.

Katydid

The last time I saw Ada, she was working at a dry cleaner's. I didn't even know that she was there. I was just picking up a suit, and she came around from the back, almost floating it seemed, beside the motorized carousel. She wore a green-and-white striped smock and her hair in one long braid down her back.

"Hey," she said. "I thought that was you."

"Wow," I said. "It's great to see you." It wasn't a lie exactly, but it wasn't as if I had known that she was there, or as if we had stayed in touch much since that summer. The clothes were swaying gently on thin hangers behind her. "How have you been?" I asked. "You look good."

"I'm okay," she said. "I got rid of Roy."

"Yeah?" I said. "How did you know?"

She laughed. "Yeah, he was on the road *a lot*." She crossed her arms in front of her body, looking a little past me. "We lived with his cousins, you know? And then he wanted us to get our own place, so I packed everything up, and the day we were going to move he didn't show up."

"Oh god," I said. "Just like—"

I stopped myself but she knew what I was going to say. Two minutes with Ada and I'm already regretting my words.

"Duane," she said. "I know."

"I'm sorry," I said. I wanted to say *sorry for Roy and sorry for Duane and sorry for what I said, just now and before; I'm sorry, sorry, sorry.* She smiled faintly and reached for the carbon receipt book.

"Hey, I can give you my discount," she said, flipping it open and sliding the cardstock flap under the carbon. I wondered how many times she'd performed this exact set of tasks, how long she'd been ringing people up, giving them discounts, plucking their sweaters and drapes off the carousel.

"Uh, thanks, but you don't need to do that," I said, fishing in the side pocket of my purse. "I have a coupon. Twenty percent." I produced the paper.

"My discount is better. Twenty-five."

I felt her eyes on me. I felt the weight of my watch on my wrist. I wanted to say, *It was a gift. The watch*, but what sense would that make? So I said thanks that would be great.

I owed her twelve dollars. She rang it up and asked about my life.

"Still cleaning teeth," I said. "That's good. Nice and calm at the office. Pays the bills."

"You still with that Norwegian?"

"Swede. Remember? 'Never—' "

"Never go with a Swede!' " And we laughed at the private joke between me, Ada, and *Love Medicine* fans everywhere.

"No," I answered. "That's done."

"I thought so. I saw him, and it wasn't with you."

I nodded. Ada was about the fiftieth person to mention this to me. "I heard about that," I said.

"Aw, Bert," she sighed. "Don't feel bad. That guy was a cold fish."

I had to smile at that.

"You have a new man now?"

"No one special," I told her, which was true.

Ada cast a sideways glance at my dry-cleaning order. Two men's shirts and a suit. She looked back at me and raised her right eyebrow.

"It's for my boss," I said, which was also true.

"Overtime's a bitch," she said.

We both laughed a little, and I asked her for her number.

I carried her phone number around for a long time after that, in the pocket of my wallet where I usually keep my fortunes. A TRUE FRIEND IS EVER TRUTHFUL. HARD TIMES ARE NOW BE-HIND YOU. IN THREE MONTHS YOU WILL RECEIVE GOOD NEWS. YOUR LUCKY NUMBER: 5.

This is the truth: Ada and I used to be close. But that was before Oklahoma, before the road trip, before our friendship became collateral damage in her father's war against himself. Or perhaps it was a drive-by in a street war, or any one of a hundred Indian wars going on at any given moment. Friendly fire cannot be ruled out. Time has not clarified what happened that summer or why, or how to mend it.

Ada was the first real friend I made when I came to Salem, having freshly emancipated myself from my previous life. We met at the All Nations Community Center, a place that, among other things, held the urban Indians together with salmon and protests, beadwork and a drum. At first, I wasn't sure how to fit in, being on my own with no family. I took my cues from Ada, who was still in high school but close to my age. She knew her way around the community because she'd grown up there, and she became my way in. Ada was kind that way. She saw the orphans and took them in. The two of us would work in the kitchen, washing dishes,

mashing potatoes, laughing with the older ladies, and getting out of the way when told.

Then the drum would start, and Ada would drop her apron for a shawl.

Ada rocked the fancy shawl and she knew it. She was a slender girl with a light step and graceful wings. When the drum started, she would wrap her arms in her shawl and placidly close her eyes. The fringe would swing and whisper, then settle as she stood perfectly still, still as a tomb. Then, right when the beat hardened, her wings would fly open and she would lift and turn, coming back to life, just as the story goes. The dance floor rolled like a field of butterflies then, her blue shawl the shimmering promise of spring.

Watching her from the kitchen, I wished that I could fly, too. I had, very recently, left my redneck hometown in a rather colorful fashion. By "colorful" I only mean salacious, good for local gossip. I didn't burn down any buildings on the way out or anything like that.

Alas, we all have regrets.

I was just nineteen and scared to be alone, but there was no way I was going back. I had made my way to Salem, which to me was a real city, and the first thing I tried to do was "find my tribe," as the hippies say. Hippies love to glorify the tribe, which is both amusing and irritating to me. If you're going to go tribal, you can't just take the good—the sharing, the ceremonies, the aunties, the Rez cred—you got to go the whole way. You got to walk through the minefields. You got to take the pettiness, the jealousy, the physical abuse, the diabetes, the bigoted uncle, the family that hates your family since the missionaries arrived. If you're a woman, you got to accept that your body is prime real

estate, and if you don't reproduce for the tribe, you've joined the occupation.

Ada and I bonded over the reproductive imperative, seeing that we were of that age and there was no way around it. She was solidly dedicated to the cause, which is probably why she put up with Roy for so long. I couldn't seem to find an Indian man to put up with. I envied her and worried about her, and she felt the same for me.

Three summers ago, Ada and I shared a mutual need to take a road trip to Pawnee, Oklahoma, for the Fourth of July Home-coming Powwow. She wanted to find her Indian relatives and I wanted to spend a week lying awake at night on the floor of a double-wide, waiting for the heat and the roar of katydids to lift. More to the point, I wanted to do for Ada what she had done for me, which was to clear a path when I needed it. Some things were uncomfortable and some things were beautiful, and some things were both. In Oklahoma we saw things we'd never seen before: armadillos, fireflies, scissor-tailed flycatchers. Comanche Nation license plates. An all–Indian line of customers at the post office. And Ada saw her grandmother's smile, and the gnarled hands of her grandfather, and a whole pageant of disappointment that only a lifetime of imagining your family can produce.

We were washing dishes at Culture Night when this whole plan got hatched. Ada was saying that she had just seen her bio-dad Duane in a recent episode of *Dr. Quinn, Medicine Woman* and that he had a part on *Walker, Texas Ranger* coming up soon.

"You're the only person I know who, when people talk about TV dads, could say, 'My TV dad is my *actual* dad,'" I said.

"Yeah, except that my dad never plays a dad on TV," she said. "Or in real life."

"Well, it's not like there's an Indian *Cosby Show*. Although that would be awesome. The dad would work for Indian Health Service and the mom would be a lawyer at NARF, and they would be ostentatiously middle class."

"What about the sweaters?"

"Right. The dad would have a huge collection of loud ribbon shirts."

We riffed on this for a while. It's surprising how much material can be mined from making Indian versions of things. Or perhaps it's not surprising. Making Indian versions of things is a time-honored skill, like cornhusk weaving or cooking with rocks.

I confess to Ada what I'd never told anyone: that my TV dad was Michael Landon from *Little House on the Prairie*. Like my own father, Pa was handsome and white and a hardworking farmer, who wanted more than anything to have a son. He was admired by the townsfolk and loved by his wife. But unlike my father, Pa forgave and helped his children when they made mistakes and broke the rules, and sometimes he even laughed at their misdeeds. He did not punish them for being willful; he never hit them or locked them in closets or pressed their faces against the wall and told them that they were *good for nothing*. He did not fill the little house with his backhand or his howl, so that the children would run outside and beg the trees to hide them.

I don't say this to her; I just confess that Michael Landon is my TV dad, and it's my Secret Shame. She laughs and promises not to tell anyone.

Eventually we came back around to Duane, and I ask Ada

if she has plans to meet him, now that she was graduating high school, or if that would be too weird for her adoptive family.

"No, they're cool with that," she said. She said she'd thought about trying to go to the Fourth of July Homecoming Powwow in Pawnee, because Duane usually stopped by that way. Being the itinerant type, he would regularly circle through Oklahoma, because apparently Pawnee is right on the path between Hollywood, where he got bit parts, and Edmonton, the far end of the Plains powwow circuit.

"Your dad is old school," I said. "He's gotta roam."

Ada was drying a giant stockpot at that moment. "Yeah," she sighed, setting it down on the counter. I picked it up and carried it to the cabinet. When I came back, she was in the same spot, holding the dishless towel in her hands, and staring out the window.

"We can roam, too," I said.

The last time I saw Ada, it was about a year ago, at the dry cleaner's. I was picking up a suit and some shirts for my boss, Rafael Cloud, and I didn't know that she would be there. Rafa ran the only Indian-owned dentistry office in the city, perhaps the State. I had volunteered for the pickup because it had been an unusually hectic Saturday and Rafa couldn't get away, and his wife was out of town, and he needed his suit to go to church on Sunday. So it was this combination of unusual circumstances that led me to Ada.

After, when I stopped at his house intending only to drop off the suit, the coupon, and the change, Rafa invited me to join them for dinner. I wasn't expecting it but I wasn't surprised either—it appeared only as Indian hospitality to me. Rafa's two boys were freshly showered and doing their homework at the kitchen table.

Their house felt cheerful and warm, and I had no other plans. Rafa made a cup of tea for me, and I sat in a stool at the kitchen island, watching him mine bones from the side of a salmon. I told him about seeing Ada and about our Oklahoma road trip, but I didn't tell him how things had fallen apart with her, or how much I missed her.

For some reason, we ended up talking about Termination. He told me how psychologically and spiritually damaging it had been for his tribe, the Klamath, to one day receive letters saying that they were no longer Indian. I knew what Termination was, but Rafa's stories were the closest I had ever come to understanding how it might have felt, how deeply existential it was, for an entire tribe to be shattered like that.

Between these stories, we shared roasted salmon so tender it melted on our tongues. We told other stories too, and made jokes and laughed with the boys. It was the first time I'd ever had what I would call a personal conversation with Rafa. It was also the first time I'd ever done anything for him outside of the office, and the first time, technically, that I'd ever touched his clothes.

And because these things happened this way, the story of my loss of Ada and my life with Rafa became braided together, so that I could no longer separate what I felt for each of them.

The spring before we went to Oklahoma, Ada mowed lawns, took on extra babysitting, pooled all of her graduation gift money, and sold enough peyote-stitch keychains to buy a $300 round-trip airline ticket to Tulsa, plus gifts for her Oklahoma family. At Culture Night, folks made and gave us beaded earrings and bolo ties to take for gifting. Roy came through with some men's chokers and two beaded medicine bags. I pulled my $300 ticket out of my

savings account, and her parents, who didn't have much to spare, offered to pay the cost of the rental car. The Drum at the community center gave us an honor song, and folks pressed tobacco bundles and small amounts of cash into our hands, telling us we were doing a good thing. As the Drum sounded, I was struck by the durability of Indian ways. Each small gesture, each prayer, each bit of food or wrinkle of cash in the palm—these elements combined to make a path for us. Once we made it to Oklahoma, we would stay with her grandparents and cousins in Pawnee, and her dad would meet up with us at the Fourth of July Homecoming Powwow. Her family, to celebrate the reunion, would even hold a Special for her.

We had tobacco and gifts and medicine from the Drum. We had cash for expenses and a credit card for emergencies. We had the prayers of mothers, healers, strangers, and kin. But was it enough? Was it enough to deliver us safely there and back?

Two days before we left, a letter arrived from my mother. I could feel the weight in the padded envelope and opened it carefully. A small pewter disk fell into my hand. In the letter she said that if she had known I was going to leave home those years ago she would have given it to me then. There was no judgment in her words about me leaving. I felt her love and her need to protect me with some power beyond herself.

I looked carefully at the disk, even though I had seen it all my life. It was her St. Christopher medal, carried by her for so long that the imprint of the saint and his dog were nearly worn away.

I closed my fist around the disk and prayed. I said the only prayer I knew: the *Nú·nim Pist.* I wasn't even sure what the words

were in English, but the cadence of Nez Perce made me feel calm and close to my mother. I could hear her voice.

My mother was Catholic and unbreakable. Like a lot of Indians, she didn't believe in God but she believed in the saints, and this faith, along with the *Nú·nim Pist*, was the only part of her religion that she passed on to us. She loved that each saint had special spiritual powers and could help you if you asked. She adored the saints like favorite uncles and aunts, and Kateri she loved the most of all. The saints could get you through anything, she said, because their power came through their trials.

The saints offered protection, empathy, and aid, but even more than that, they offered something that could really deliver: perspective. The saints *suffered*. No matter what you may face, they definitely had it worse than you, so you can quit feeling sorry for yourself and buck up. Nothing makes quite the impression as a saint carrying his own severed head in his hands.

I slid the medal into my pocket. I carried it to Oklahoma and back, and for a long time after that. The first time I kissed Rafa I had that medal in my pocket. It was a long time after our summer in Oklahoma. But I still believed in it, and I carried it with as much faith as I ever had in anything.

"Ada, I have a confession," I told her the morning we left for Tulsa, as we strapped in to our plane seats. She leaned closer. "I've never been on a plane before."

"It's okay," she said. "I haven't either."

"Are you scared?"

"No. Are you?"

"No. People fly all the time."

"I'm never scared," Ada said. "And I never cry either."

Coming from someone else, I might not have believed it. But Ada was a foster kid, and then an adopted kid living in a foster home. She'd seen people come and go her whole life, so when she said *never* I believed it.

I never felt the air so thick as I did getting off the plane in Tulsa. Ada and I waited at the carousel for her one piece of checked baggage to appear: a Pendleton box wrapped tight with packing tape, carrying the Circle of Life blanket she had bought for her grandparents. It was a blinding ninety-seven degrees and humid, and the last thing I wanted to see, touch, or carry was a wool blanket. But Ada let out a deep breath when she saw the box drop onto the conveyor belt, and her relief made me think she probably was scared sometimes—not scared of a plane crash, but scared to come home without a gift. Afraid that a lifetime away from kin had made her irredeemable. Aside from the blanket, we were traveling light, each of us with a small bag of clothes. We'd boarded the plane on a chilly Oregon morning and were sweltering at midday in our jeans in Oklahoma. Ada wore her hair in two tight braids; I imagined her mom carefully plaiting each side as the light quietly slipped through the kitchen windows of their suburban house. I pulled my hair up in a ponytail, to keep it off my neck in the heat and to better show off the earrings Ada had made for me.

We had instructions to drive ourselves to the Pawnee IGA parking lot and call Ada's grandfather from there. Along the highway I was surprised at how lush the grasses grew. The waterways were muddy and brown, but that didn't seem to bother the hawks and turkey vultures circling overhead. The earth radiated the color of brick.

"Look! Pawnee County!" Ada exclaimed as we passed the county line sign. And then, as we came into town, she recited everything she saw with the word *Pawnee* on it. *Pawnee Municipal Swimming Pool! Pawnee High School! Pawnee Video! Pawnee Lake!* Her whole life in Oregon she had been alone, saying the word *Pawnee* to other people, explaining herself: *I'm Pawnee; I'm adopted.* And suddenly she was here, where that word spoke back to her. All around: Pawnee, Pawnee, Pawnee. And at the end of Sewell, just past Moses Yellowhorse Drive, the Pawnee IGA.

After she called, we sat with the windows rolled down in the car, inviting the thick breeze to cool our skin and nerves. Waiting. Ada occupied herself by tapping her hand on the dash and singing to herself, an Omaha intertribal that was a favorite of Roy's drum. She gazed across the parking lot at the bins of watermelon and displays of fireworks that clustered around the doors of the IGA. I felt invisible to her, and to be honest I wanted to disappear, to dissolve into the body of a night heron or a fox, to be a quiet, unseen observer. Perhaps waiting wouldn't be so hard that way.

At work each morning I tidy up the waiting room. Often there isn't much to do, just straighten the rows of magazines, or pick up a stray scrap that the building cleaning crew has missed. I rather like to putter around the waiting room. A large medicine wheel is painted on the wall, and the chairs are upholstered with authentic Pendleton fabric, custom-made at no small expense. Still, as pleasant and culturally affirming as that room was, some folks hate it no matter what you do. Waiting can be unpleasant, not because of duration but intensity. In our case, on that day, we were waiting in the parking lot for Ada's life to change, for her question to be answered, for her arms and her life to come full circle in the

embrace of her long-lost family. Would some part of her recognize them, or would they remain foreign, or something in between?

Waiting is harder when you know you are doing it. When I first felt Rafa's hand on my body, I did not know until I felt it that I had been waiting, even longing, for it. His touch was innocent enough, just a light touch, almost accidental. "Roberta," he said, coming up behind me, touching my elbow with his hand, "can you bring me the X-ray for that impacted bicuspid?"

No one falls in love with a man for saying *impacted bicuspid*, which should only make the point that it was his touch that awakened me. For three years I had worked with him, the only Indian dentist or doctor I'd ever known, the only man I'd ever known who owned an actual suit instead of a Western-style sport coat. Like me, Rafa was mixed: his father was Klamath and his mother was Filipina and his wife was white and his children were beautiful. And this is the truth. I knew it was wrong to want him, but one day my heart flew away and I ran after it.

Ada's grandfather had bright eyes, a worn, wrinkled face, and a slow, deliberate body. In his seventies, his hair was salt-and-pepper gray, with substantial swaths of coarse black strands. He wore denim overalls and a slate work shirt, and a scuffed pair of Red Wing boots. When he arrived in his blue Ford F-150 at the Pawnee IGA, he killed the engine and slipped out of the cab, smiling. Ada jumped out of the car and ran to him. They hugged each other briefly, stiffly, as I withdrew from the car to join them. We exchanged some greetings, then he told us to follow him home. Without saying a word, Ada bounded to the passenger side of his truck and climbed in, turning back to wave at me, a happy bird.

The asphalt road that led to their family home deposited us

on a dirt driveway in front of a battered double-wide with a large wooden deck built on front. Ada's grandma was seated there on a fold-up style picnic chair, wearing a floral-print cotton skirt and a bright yellow T-shirt, drinking a Diet Coke. As soon as we arrived, a cluster of grown-up cousins, aunties, and small children emerged from various points: the front and back screen doors, the hood of a 1980s Volvo sedan, the clump of trees that shaded the house. I stood back, watching the circle form around Ada, each one smiling, laughing, and embracing her. Ada's uncle and auntie, Jesse and Max, and their four little children lived in the house with the grandparents. Nan, the older sister of Duane, lived in Oklahoma City with her two teenage daughters. When Nan greeted Ada, she told her that it was really a homecoming, a return home, because Ada's mom, Daisy, had been there when she was pregnant. This was news to Ada, who had never heard much about her birth mom, except that she was a poor white girl who in 1978, the year Ada was born, believed her baby would have a better life elsewhere.

After the initial welcome, everyone seemed to forget about us. The kids went back to playing in the yard, Jesse returned to the Volvo, and the grandma resumed her place on the porch, watching over the kids. Over the next few days, we fell somewhat awkwardly into the patterns of the family, eating in shifts, sleeping on the floor, and taking daily excursions into town, picking up pieces of family stories as they appeared before us.

Nan said that Daisy was perfectly named because she was a real flower child. She had come home with Duane pregnant, then she stayed with his family even after he left. Four months. And then she disappeared. Maybe she went back to her own people, Nan said, and Ada shrugged her shoulders.

Ada's grandfather opened his left hand to show Ada a deep

scar that ran across his palm, the result of a horse-riding injury as a teenager, when he worked for Pawnee Bill's Wild West Show. Several of his fingers had been broken, too, and never quite healed right. One day we drove out with Nan and her daughters to Pawnee Bill's Ranch and toured his mansion. On the grounds Ada was just as surprised to see antelope and buffalo herds as groups of white tourists who stared at us.

The pace of life in Pawnee reminded me of my own childhood, minus the chores and the livestock. I grew up rural, but not on the Rez, and not anywhere near Colville, geographically speaking. My mom had married a white farmer, and that's how we ended up in the sticks of Idaho. My dad was constitutionally an angry person, and sharp-witted as hell. As I've grown older, I've come to see how often those characteristics come packaged together. He was rough, but my mother was calm, and her words were the cool waters that kept us afloat in a town that didn't much care for her or us. No surprise, but I got out of there the first second I could.

These days, I suppose a sociologist would call me an urban Indian, but in Salem we were suburban Indians at best. And if I had to be honest about where I came from, I'd have to explain all those years of moving irrigation pipe and bottle-feeding lambs. Basically I'm a farm Indian, a demographic absurdity: half Nez Perce, quarter 4-H, quarter Coors Longneck.

In Pawnee, we kept busy every day, despite not having a lot to do. Ada dutifully threaded a whole package of needles for her grandma, and delighted in calling her Meemaw, just like her Oklahoma cousins did. We made beaded earrings, went swimming at

the local pool, drove to town for groceries, watched game show reruns, and dodged long yellow spirals of fly strips hanging from every room in the trailer. One afternoon, on a quiet asphalt road, I let Ada drive our rental car. I was with her of course, but I'm pretty sure that putting her behind the wheel for the first time was breaking my role as a responsible party.

Every day Ada would learn more about her Pawnee family. And every day she'd hear the same report about her father: Duane was on the way. He had just called from Standing Rock. Next outpost had him at Dupree.

Don't worry, he said. He would be home in time for the Special.

This is the truth: I tried, at first, to resist my thoughts about Rafa.

I planted his wife, Janice, in my mind. I thought about their children. I knew I had no right to him, not really. But I couldn't control my thoughts at night. Other worlds would open and I would dream of him, and rise from my bed feeling that he belonged to me. Alone, I would close my eyes and remember his touch on my elbow. At work, I began to ration small indulgences. I would allow myself to observe him, at first just once a day. I would see him focus on the details of molars and gums, how steadily he would peer into the mouth of a patient. His gaze drew me in.

As the dentist studies the mouth, so the lover examines the world of his beloved.

I began to long for his impartial, diagnostic eye for the good, the bad, and the damaged to turn upon me, upon my face, my life, my soul. This is how I longed for Rafa to look upon me, and I on him. At Christmas he gave each of his employees a watch as a gift. The first time I put it on my wrist I recalled the weight of

his touch on my skin. I tried not to wonder if Janice had picked out the watch. The weight of the watch was a comfort to me, and I decided that it would be all that I would have of his affection.

Still, I fed the ache.

There were times I wanted Rafa's kiss so much I felt I could push down a wall. But I would do nothing. I would only wish, and wait and wait and wait.

One night, the night before he was to arrive, Ada and I were lying on the floor of the living room, unable to sleep. The heat lay down with us, the flies buzzed loudly and smacked against the strips, and the crickets and katydids droned around us. We had no pillows, no blankets. We just lay on the floor in our clothes every night, propping up our heads with extra folded T-shirts. So we were there, staring at the ceiling, and I asked Ada if she wanted to hear a story that my auntie from Lapwai told me. She did. Well, I said. It goes like this.

A woman, a man, and her mother were traveling. They stopped to camp one night, and the wife said to her husband, "No matter what you do, do not talk about the katydids."

They set up their camp, and they made dinner. The katydids sang around them, but the husband said nothing. They ate. And then, as they were getting ready for bed, the husband said, "The katydids are very loud tonight."

And his mother-in-law heard him. She jumped up from where she was and threw a blanket around her shoulders like a cape. She began to run in circles and to sing. She wanted to join the katydids. No matter what the wife said, the mother could not hear her. She only sang louder.

The wife was upset. "Look what you've done!" she said to her

husband. "I told you not to mention the katydids. My mother is a katydid, and now she wants to fly away with them."

The mother sang and sang and sang. There was nothing the husband and wife could do. The woman longed to return to the katydids, and she couldn't stop singing; she sang and sang and sang until she sang herself to death.

That's all.

"That's a good story," Ada said.

"Yes," I said. "But it's too short for a long night."

One night, a few months after I first kissed Rafa, I asked him to tell me the story of his name.

"My mother named me," he said. "Rafael. For the angel." He smiled slightly, then his brow furrowed a bit. We were lying close in bed, my bed, as always. "You know the archangels? Michael, Gabriel, Uriel, Raphael." He said their names carefully. Then he lifted his hand to my cheek and kissed me. Rafa has full lips and a gentle kiss, and I pressed my body against his. I said I did not know the angels. I wrapped my leg around his, wanting to claim him.

"No?" he said. "Michael and Gabriel are messengers. Uriel is the protector." He touched my shoulder, then pulled his hand away. He rested it on the bed, in the space between us. "Raphael is the healer."

"You had to be a doctor then," I said, and placed my hand on his.

"I don't think that was it," he said, leaning a bit away from me. "I think it was her two miscarriages before me. *Ay, Dios.* So

many times she told us. Besides," he said, "People don't think of us as healers." He kissed me again. "Dentists are more like maintenance workers. Mechanics."

"Dentists are priests," I said. "People come to confess. They cannot hide their sins; they don't want to. *Forgive me, Father, for I have not flossed.*" I placed both hands on my heart for dramatic effect. I wasn't sure how people confessed, but I continued anyway. "*It has been more than six months since my last cleaning. Have mercy on me,*" I said. "*Remove from me this burden of plaque.*" I paused, realizing that I could be insulting Rafa's religion, his mother, his profession, or all three at once, but Rafa's eyes were playful.

"Save me," I said.

Rafa placed his hand on my head. "My child, you are forgiven. Go," he said, "And sin no more. Also: don't forget to floss."

"Rafael," I said. He looked at me, his face curious, waiting for me to continue. But I had nothing to say, nothing to ask.

We woke up groggy and tired on the morning of the Fourth of July. "My dad is coming today," Ada said, as though I had forgotten the purpose of our visit. I gave her a quick one-armed hug. We stumbled to the kitchen and poured ourselves some cereal. We were sitting on the porch in our sunglasses and shorts, drinking weak coffee, when Nan's car rumbled up the dirt road. She asked us to come to town with her. Ada jumped up to go, and I said I'd like to stay behind.

"Both of you," Nan said, and I heard the edge in her voice. We made small talk on the way. Grand Entry for the powwow was at 1:00 p.m. The IGA was closing early today. Jesse and Max were up all night finishing a pair of moccasins for their youngest daughter.

We pulled into the IGA and Nan turned to Ada, holding out a five. "Get a gallon of milk and some sparklers for the kids."

As soon as the glass doors slid shut behind Ada, Nan turned to me. "Duane is not coming."

"Shit," I said. "Why?"

Nan pressed her lips tight and looked straight out the windshield.

"You have to tell Ada," she said.

"*I* have to tell her? Why?"

"You know her. You brought her. It's better coming from you."

Shit, I thought. Shit, shit, shit.

I probably knew that this was going to happen, not that this would make me particularly prescient. I mean, do the math: (Girl − Dad) + 18 years = No Show. There would be no Special either. I wondered if Ada had already suspected. Probably not, I thought. Not much evidence, really. There have been a few times I'd seen a Give Away come together in hours rather than weeks or years, so the fact that there hadn't been much visible activity on that front wasn't conclusive. But did they all know that Duane wouldn't come? These were my thoughts as we drove back to the house, the sun bearing down and the trees motionless for lack of wind. I watched rows of heat waves lift from the surface of red earth and release into the sky.

Rafa had two boys, and thinking of them, while meant to be preventative, fed my hunger instead. At first it worked. It worked way better than thinking about his wife. At first all I could think was how it would hurt them—how *I* would hurt them—if their father

pulled away. What would it mean to break up an Indian family just to have an Indian man? But then, because I had allowed myself to draw out this scenario, I found another way down that path. I began to imagine him with me, and *them* with me. I would recall that night at their house, eating salmon and talking at the table. I saw how perfect it could be to slip into a ready-made family. Often the boys would come by the office at the end of the school day, after basketball practice, and do their homework. Sometimes Janice would pick them up or drop them off. But I wanted to be very careful with my desire, to hide it.

Culture Night at All Nations became awkward, and the place where I most feared exposure. When Rafa came to Culture Night with his boys, I would keep myself busy in the kitchen.

But one night I saw that Janice brought the boys. The next week, she did it again.

And that was when I saw the pattern. It had been a long time since I saw all four of them together. Janice and Rafa were like two elevators, side by side, and the boys were getting on and off. One day, just before Christmas, I overheard Rafa say he was taking the boys to Klamath for the holidays, and Janice was going to her family. I saw it very clearly then, that there was an opening, and I knew if I waited long enough, and if I let on to him just enough, the doors would slide open for me, and I could go on.

The clock was ticking, and I had to tell Ada. Grand Entry was only hours away. Back at the trailer, she was making cheese sandwiches for the kids in the kitchen.

I called to her from the door. She came out.

We sat together on the steps of the deck. I wasn't sure what to say. She was wearing mirrored sunglasses and I felt self-conscious

of my own reflection as she looked at me. I clutched the St. Christopher medal tight in my fist.

"Ada," I said. "You made your family happy by coming here. And I think this won't be the only time you're here with them."

She nodded. A dog barked in the distance.

"Dads can be . . . unpredictable," I said. "I mean, really unpredictable. Or maybe totally predictable. My dad . . . his unpredictability was the most predictable thing about him. You would do something, and there was no way to know what he would do. He drank a lot. Too much. When I left home, I just wanted to get away from him, to get free. And he is . . . um, white. A white man."

I could see her eyebrows crease behind her glasses.

"Dads can fail you," I said. "They can hurt you. But it's about them, and not about you."

"Okay," she said. Her face recovered a placid expression.

I breathed out. "Duane isn't coming."

"I know," she said. Her face did not change.

I wondered whether this was true.

We sat there in silence, unmoving. A breeze suddenly stirred the cottonwood trees, and the shudder of leaves reminded me of home.

"I'm sorry," I said, and placed my hand on her knee.

She allowed my hand to rest there a moment. Then she pushed it away. She stood. She took a few steps toward the kitchen. She stopped, turned her head, and spoke over her shoulder, her words swift and brittle.

"Your dad's effed up," she said, "but mine isn't."

She did not cry. And she did not speak. We rode to the powwow grounds in silence, and I felt the river between us widen, like a

delta opening to the sea. At the powwow, we fell into familiar rituals of work: setting up the dance arbor, hauling picnic chairs from the cars, fetching ice for the coolers, bringing in gallons of water for the dancers and snacks for the kids. In this way, we circled around our wounds and each other.

That afternoon, Ada danced the fancy shawl at the Fourth of July Homecoming Powwow. I watched from the side, still the interloper in her family's arbor. I felt a foreigner too, in the world of Oklahoma Indians. Even at Sho-Ban Days I had never seen such a spectacular Grand Entry, with more than a thousand dancers in feathers and beadwork, spiraling and moving in time to the drum. Beads of sweat flew from the cheeks and arms of the fancy dancers, and rolled in steady streaks down the faces of the jingle and grass dancers. Rows of stately older ladies moved as one, managing the sway of their fringed shawls and dresses *just so*. The air was thick, yet clouds were distant. Our coolers were filled with ice, and we sucked on the cubes and rubbed them across our collarbones and shoulders for relief.

I looked around me and saw only the faces of strangers. I wanted to dissolve into the sound of the drum, the only thing that felt familiar to me in that moment. Ada's distance gnawed at me. When the Fancy Shawl category was called, I watched her glide out to her spot on the edge of the circle, wrapping herself tight in her blue shawl. Her grandparents watched from their lawn chairs. The crowhop started, and Ada lifted with the beat. I wondered if she felt at home, dancing in this place. I wondered if I had brought her more pain or less.

I thought about her mother, Daisy. *A real flower child.* Daisy was an outsider, too. I wondered if she had stood in this very spot, in this same dance arbor, feeling the world spiral around her. Did she feel as alone then as I did? I wished that Daisy could see Ada

now, could see how things came full circle. I found some comfort in this thought.

We are Salmon People, I said to myself. We always circle back. But at that moment, I was slipping into the ocean.

I felt Ada move away from me. That night, she wanted to stay for the 49, and she made it clear that she would go with her cousins, not me. But I could not leave her there alone. I fell asleep in the parking lot, in the back seat of our rental car, even while the fireworks exploded overhead. Sometime during the night, she got in the car, wearing shorts and beadwork and the smell of smoke and sweat. The next morning the sun glowed orange through the windows, and we lifted our stiff bodies to drive back to the trailer, where we washed our faces in the sink and quietly gathered up our bags. Later she said *goodbye* and *love you* and *see you soon* to her family, and I said *thank you* to everyone. We flew back to Salem, and we told everyone that we had a wonderful time. For some reason, folks at Culture Night didn't ask about her dad, and we didn't volunteer. Ada and I held that secret together.

But we were never close again. Whenever I think of her now, I remember her in that circle, her arms open and her feet light.

Rafa asked me why I didn't just call her. He made it sound easy and natural, yet neither of those things were true. Almost a year had gone by since I saw her last, that day at the dry cleaner's. It felt like too much time. But Rafa knew how I missed her, and he wasn't one to give up. *She gave you her number*, he reminded me.

She gave up on me, I reminded him.

—

Sometimes I think love is a trap, sometimes a promise, sometimes a physics problem. Whether faith is gravity or the ability to fly is still an open question. It seems that it should be easier to chart, easier to calculate: how one loss blooms into another, how one moment of connection is a crash and another is deliverance. Desire is its own force, bringing people into our orbit and flinging our hearts far beyond our bodies, so that we have no choice but to follow.

It was true that of all the heartaches I had felt in my life, the strange disintegration of my friendship with Ada was the worst. I longed to talk with her. I missed her company in the All Nations kitchen. The private jokes I wanted to share with her were piling up, unused, like a bag of clothes to be taken to Goodwill. Sometimes I thought I understood what happened: A combination of her need to kill the messenger and the fact that I had been a dismal messenger. Or maybe it was that I witnessed a pain she could not hide. Maybe I reminded her too much of the things that went wrong, and not of the good. Maybe it was me.

Perhaps I protected my heart, or at least I tried to, when I thought about calling her, which was every day.

Still, I had to do something. I arranged a small altar beside my bed: abalone shell, sage and sweetgrass. An eagle feather from my auntie. A Kateri medal on a silver chain. Ada's phone number. St. Christopher and his Dog. And from Oklahoma: a bundle of tobacco wrapped in red cloth.

—

Rafa said it wasn't enough. *It's not enough to hope and wait.*

So I called her one day and left a message.

Nothing.

But not long after that, three things happened all at once: I opened the door for Rafa, I handed him the test stick, and the phone rang. Before I could speak, he drew me tight in his arms, and I let the machine pick up the call. It was Ada.

"Bert," she said. "Are you there?"

Her voice sounded small.

Rafa pulled back. *You should pick up,* he said.

I grabbed the receiver and switched off the machine. "Ada? Are you okay?"

I lowered myself to the edge of the sofa, gesturing to Rafa to sit beside me. I wanted him close.

"Yes," she said. "No."

"What happened?"

"Meemaw died."

"Oh, Ada," I said. "I'm sorry."

"That's not the worst part," she said.

My mind raced to think what could be worse.

"They didn't tell me," she said, and her words came faster: "It happened a month ago, and they didn't tell me. I found out because I called them."

"Oh no," I said. "I'm so sorry."

A mix of anger and sadness spread through my chest. If Duane had gone home for the funeral, they would have needed to keep Ada away.

The line was silent. Then I heard her fighting to catch her breath. She was crying.

I didn't know what to say, and I was afraid of saying the wrong thing.

"She loved you," I said. This made her cry harder.

You should go, Rafa mouthed to me. I glanced at the white stick that lay on the table, its bright red sign screaming for attention.

"Ada, what can I do?" I asked.

She didn't answer, but her breath seemed to slow. Rafa began to pantomime *I. Drive. You.*

We stayed on the line together. I almost did not want to move. Yet I knew that I had to.

Rafa stood up and made more elaborate gestures: *You. Go.*

"I don't know," she said.

I felt her slip away from me.

"You should go," Rafael said, this time out loud. "I'll take you."

"Wait," I said into the phone. "Wait."

For a moment there was only the sound of the three of us breathing and the rain pounding the roof. My eyes were locked with Rafa's, and his gaze was steady.

"Can I come over?" I asked. "Or can you come here?"

"When?" she asked. "Tonight? Or ... "

It was pouring out, dark and cold.

"Tonight," I said, trying not to sound anxious. "We'll have tea. I really want to see you."

She was quiet; she had stopped crying. I was afraid she would say *no* and hang up. My words rushed out then, like they were trying to catch her.

"I want to talk to you," I said. "There's something I need to tell you. I'm ... "

I couldn't finish the sentence, but she did.

"You're pregnant?" she asked.

"Yes," I said. "How did you know?"

"I don't know. That's just how that sentence usually ends."

"*'I'm'* usually ends with *'pregnant'*?"

"When you say it like that it does. "

"How did I say it?"

"Like you're pregnant. Like you had really big news."

"Yeah," I said. "It is big." Rafa smiled at me. We had yet to talk about it. "You're the first person I've told," I said. "I mean, the second. I just found out."

"It's awesome, Bert," she said. Rafa sat down again beside me. Ada asked when the baby was due and I said I wasn't sure, that it had only been a month or maybe just a few weeks. She paused upon hearing this. I wondered if we shared the same thought: *interesting timing.* In this opening I asked her again about getting together. I told her again that I was sorry about her grandma. I offered again to make tea. I asked again if she would come here, or if I could go there. I said I thought we could both use some company. I said I wanted to talk about Meemaw. I said, *will you please come?*

Yes, she said, *I'm on my way*, and I said, *see you soon*. Then I hung up the phone and threw my arms around Rafael.

We talk for only a short while about the baby. Plans for the future would come later. Rafa offers to leave so that I can have time alone with Ada. *Call me when she leaves and I will come back*, he says. I tell him that it may be late, and he says it doesn't matter.

I will come back, he says, and I know that he will.

At the door, he kisses me and we hold each other for a long time. When he goes, I close the door carefully behind him. Now

I'm waiting for Ada, listening to the rain, feeling the heartbeat of the world in my body.

I'm putting the kettle on the stove for tea when I hear Ada knock at the door, then her voice call out from the other side.

Do you hear that? I say to myself, to the baby, as I walk toward the door. *Your auntie arrives.*

netí·telwit / human beings

without mercy the Cayuse and Nez Perce through their own country. The Cayuse brother, Polynaikas, was riding out ahead of the others. His father was already dead. His mother and his grandmothers and all their kin were starving. The people were running north, following deer trails and old routes and new allies to a land beyond the Blue Coats' reach. Polynaikas was hardly more than a boy, but he rode as a man, rode his horse toward the Medicine Line on a cold autumn day. The Crows saw him and set the Blue Coats upon him. The Blue Coat General Cut Arm himself chased after Polynaikas, but none could catch him. Only his own blood-brother, Ataoklas, was his equal. There in that valley the two brothers found each other, and there they tangled in each other's shields and cries and blood. They fell together there, shared blood filling the earth, darkening their homeland, the self-shared blood that flowed from their mother when they first left her body. They fell silent there, arm to arm, and colored that valley bed with the dark stain of broken brotherhood.

The sun rose over them; the sun was high and bright when the Blue Coats rode through. The Blue Coats found the brothers and took their horses. A warrior's horse should follow him to the Shadowland, but they were deprived of this rite; even the Crow brother, for his service to the Blue Coats, was not rewarded with the return of his horse on the other side. The Blue Coats stripped the brothers of their clothes, shields, medicine bundles, and war shirts adorned with beads, shells, and strands of their sisters' hair. Soon there was nothing, then, to mark one brother as Cayuse and the other brother as Crow. In a common grave the Blue Coats left them. There the brothers lay beside each other, in their homeland, blood and bone united once more, yet no one there to pray for them, no one there to drum and sing them to the Shadowland, no one to journey with them to the other side, no horses to join them there.

Did the brothers remain forever this way, twined in death? No, not long they lay there. Not many years hence the White Coats arrived. The White Coats came, rent open the earth, tore the brothers apart. The White Gloves measured, indexed, catalogued, and arranged the brothers in separate tombs that were metal drawers, gave them numbers and sealed the vaults. Now, as dawn breaks over the grounds of the museum, the sisters ANTIKONI and ISMENE stand in the exhibit hall of the building that holds their Ancestors, the brothers locked in unholy repose, along with the remains of thousands more.

ANTIKONI   Ismene, Ɂáyi,[1]
        We were born into this suffering. That our own
           blood would be divided
        From us, that our mourning could never come to an
           end, for it can never
        Properly begin. Have you heard
        The latest decree, that all are forbidden from this
           place?
        Not drum or song or sweetgrass smoke, no prayer
           may be given
        Our Ancestors here.
        And what is denied the dead is denied the living ten
           times again.
        We remain the captives with them.
        Tell me, Ɂáyi, have you heard any news? Do you feel
           our enemies
        Surround us, even those who once called them-
           selves our Friends?

---

1 "my sister" addressive kinship term for woman's younger sister

ISMENE   Né·ne'[2]

There is talk enough to go around. But now I hear
nothing, from Friend or foe.
Our status is ever precarious. Nothing has changed.
The law
Will speak however it wants.

ANTIKONI   It is in the shadow of this Hall that I called you here
alone.
It is in the shadow of this law that I speak.

ISMENE   I fear what I am about to hear.

ANTIKONI   Kreon has made a great purchase for his palace. The
warshirt of our
Ancestor, Ataoklas, has been found. Across the
ocean it was held, among the
Treasures looted from our motherland. Kreon has
bought it and plans to bring it
Back for a great display. A show of the brave Ata-
oklas, who gave his life for the
State, who killed his own kin for Manifest Dest.
The great warshirt of Ataoklas, along with his
bloody ǩáplac,[3] is to be storied in
A gleaming vitrine, while his selfsame body disar-
ticulates beneath the floor.
Kreon speaks of honor for Ataoklas, but the

2 "my sister" addressive kinship term for woman's older sister
3 war club

blood-pride of nonʔtáq[4] runs thin. He honors not
Ataoklas, nor our faithful himíyu[5] Polynaikas.
By the law of this land we cannot interfere.
We cannot touch the beadwork or leggins
    or the bodies
Brought forth by our grandmothers' labor.
There is a great penalty: prison.
Prison for those who touch the things that truly be-
    long to them, that seek rest
        For those who remain tormented.
Surely ʔáyi, you are aware of all of these things.
    Soon you will have the
Chance to show how you feel, how noble and true
    you are
To the path of nú·nim titílu.[6]

ISMENE   Né·ne', our lives are short and this problem is long.
        We cannot undo
        The designs of five hundred years. Did our Ances-
        tors survive
        So that we could throw our lives away?

ANTIKONI   I beg you to be one heart with me. And of the same
        hand.

ISMENE   What do you intend?

---

4 "our uncle" kinship term for mother's brother
5 ancestor, relative
6 "our Ancestors"

ANTIKONI   I will bring out their bodies. I cannot carry the bur-
           dens alone.

ISMENE   You know this cannot be done. Not only Kreon will
           stop you. The laws
           Will stop you. The bodies are ungoverned by us;
           they are the State's treasure
           And the jealous words of the State will snare you.

ANTIKONI   Ɂáyi, Ɂikú·yn nú·nim titílu hiwsí·x![7]
           I cannot betray them.

ISMENE   You will go against nonɁtáq then?

ANTIKONI   Why not once betray the blood who twice betrayed
           mine? Who is he to stop me?

ISMENE   Né·ne', timné·nekse.[8]
           You must hold it in your heart, do not be ruled by a
           strong head.
           Give some thought to our history.
           Our father is dead by his own hand, our mother by
           disease.
           Both could not bear their own living flesh.
           Our grandfathers and grandmothers were forced to
           boarding schools, beaten and
           assailed by brutes.

---

7 "Sister, truly they are our Ancestors!"
8 "Sister, I worry." Literally: "I think in my heart."

Our great-grandparents survived the war,
lived through the Hot Place,

    endured Leavenworth,

    and prisons filled with children.

Not so many generations back
Our people were slaughtered. Surely you must know
That these rulers have power greater than ours. If
  we defy the law,
They will make examples of us, punish us.
We are women and have more to lose: our life-
  giving, our blood. They take away children, they
  sterilize mothers. These things they have done.
Listen, né·ne', their power is greater than ours on
  this land.

(pause)

And it is not only the State who may punish you.
  But think of our kinsmen
Of other Red Nations. What will you risk of theirs?
  You may succeed in your
Dangerous quest—you may bring the lost brothers
  home.
But surely your fate will befall the others. They will
  be punished as well.
Perhaps more severely—although I fear you risk al-
  ready your life.
The Tribes will be angry if your stunt closes the door
To all others who pray for their Ancestors' remains.
Those Tribes who have papers, who are following
The rules as NAGPRA demands. They will lose if
  you succeed.

Let us work with them, with the path that is there,
    rather than forge ahead
On a doomed course.

ANTIKONI We see things differently. You will not join me in this
    action.
    Do what you will, but I will return our Ancestors
    home, to give peace
    To the living and the dead. And I will soon find this
    peace.
    I am ready for it. It is better to die a noble death
    than to live as a captive,
    Though you bear your chains lightly.
    I would die with honor for those whose honor I
    defend.
    I will commit this sacred crime, for I am true
    To the Order of the world, the eternal laws, set in
    motion
    Long before this time now, this time that will some-
    day end.

ISMENE I believe in our ways, as you do, but direct action
    Against the State is suicide. And for the Tribes there
    could be consequences.

ANTIKONI Say what you will. You will see what talk has gotten
    us in all of these years.
    I will not treaty that way—I treat with my actions.

ANTIKONI *turns to leave.*

ISMENE Né·ne', I fear for you.

ANTIKONI Fear for yourself. You accept this unholy order.

ISMENE Be quiet in what you do and I will keep your secret.

ANTIKONI I'd rather you denounced me in public as you do in private.

ISMENE You are choosing the dead over the living. You would restore the one who
Betrayed us, Ataoklas, who rode out against his own brother.
What do we owe him for that?
He made the Cavalry his kinsmen—let him sleep uneasily with them.

ANTIKONI By blood he belongs to us.

ISMENE It is wrong to be foolish with blood.

ANTIKONI You declare that you are averse to me and to our Ancestors.
We have chosen sides. I will carry ʔí·nim himíyu[9] with me from exile
To our home in the Shadowlands, across the Five Mountains.

---

9 "my Ancestors/relations"

At peace there, we will be beyond the reach of our
enemies. For this dream
I live and will die.

ANTIKONI leaves.

ISMENE I cannot stop you on this trial. But I will pray here
for you,
As for any warrior away on a quest.

ISMENE leaves. The CHORUS of five Aunties,
the counselors of Kreon, enter, wearing wing
dresses and moccasins. The leader carries a
hand DRUM, which she plays as they enter.

CHORUS *(Drumming stops. Silence.)*

AUNTIE #1 Wá·qoʔ titwatísa ná·qc.[10]
Coyote was going upriver. By chance
He came upon the Gophers, and he taught them
How to roast camas in an underground pit.
They were happy and there was much camas to eat.
One day he told them, *I want to get close to the Sun.*
So Coyote married the Five Gopher Sisters.
He married them and there he stayed for a while
with his in-laws.
Then one day he said to his wives, *Make for me a
tunnel directly to the Sun,
With holes so I can breathe.*

---

10 "Now I'm going to tell a story."

Now the father of Sun, the Old Man, lived there at
  Sun's house,
    and together they made trouble.
Every time Sun made a kill and brought it home,
The first thing the Old Man would do
    is cut off the balls
    and eat them raw.

CHORUS   Ohhhh ...

AUNTIE #1 Now Coyote was getting close to Sun's house
When suddenly:
    There was Sun!
And Coyote called out, *Little Brother!*
Sun was surprised, because his back was turned.
Coyote said again, *Little Brother,*
You are sitting in the wrong direction. You are sitting up here
  to ambush.
Over here is where our fathers—my father and your father—
  used to go,
Way back when. There's a firepit over here somewhere.
Coyote took Sun and said, *Right here it is!*
Surely here was their fire; here are arrowheads and things.
Coyote quickly dug a hole and pulled out an
  arrowhead.
And Sun believed: *Yes, surely!* he said.
From Earth's very beginning it was like this,
And this is how it always was.
Coyote says to Sun, *Now let's chase each other, Little*
  Brother.
Coyote used magic to make water pour from a spring.

Then he said to the Sun, *Let's give ourselves a drink. You
  first, Little Brother.*
Now Sun put down his war club, and Coyote said
  to him,
Stop, stop, Little Brother.
*Let's do as our fathers used to do—my father and your
  father—they would hold their war clubs for each other.*
And Coyote held the war club for Sun.
Sun put his head in the water to drink,
  and Coyote knocked him out.
  Coyote beat him,
And then Sun dropped dead.
Coyote loaded Sun on his back and carried him
  home.
Coyote traded his clothes with Sun;
  he dressed himself in Sun's clothes.
He used magic on himself, saying:
  Exactly like Sun I will become.
And that way Coyote, dressed as Sun, carried Sun
  home.
He carried Sun to his father. First thing:
  The father cut off the balls and ate them raw.
The Old Man said,
That sure was kind of bitter.
Always the father would eat like that, and then they
  would go to bed.
Outside of their tipi
A terrible thing!
A leftover skull placed in a circle.
That Old Man had all the remains they had killed
  With their skulls there in a circle.

Coyote felt uneasy.

He lay there, quietly, and soon it became night.

When the Old Man began to snore, Coyote thought
  to himself,

Ah, yes, now I will leave him.

Then   Coyote   readied   himself   and   traveled
  huuuuu ... a great distance, all night.

As dawn arrived, he thought:

Now I am far away. Right here I will take a nap.

When he woke,

    Coyote was right back where he started.

Now the Old Man came out and saw Coyote dressed
  as his Son.

He says, *Why, my Son, are you out here sleeping on the
  dancing grounds?*

(pause)

Then the Old Man says, *Yes, my little one,*

    now surely I feel death close by.

Thus it went—second night,

    third night,

        fourth night,

            to the fifth night.

Every night

    Coyote would travel long, take a nap, and wake
  up to find himself

    back at the Old Man's doorstep.

Coyote made a plan: *Just as soon as he goes to sleep,*

*Then I will cut off his head. That is the only way I could
  leave him.*

And that very thing Coyote did.

    He cut off the Old Man's head.

When he finished cutting it off, then he said to Sun:
You must be separated.
Of you it will be said: This is the light of the daytime.
  You will walk across the sky, and never again will you
    kill.
In the same way, the Old Man will be the light of the night-
    time. This one will walk across the sky
and never again eat anything raw.
The humans are coming soon.
They are already coming this way.
That's all.

FIRST EPISODE/SCENE II

KREON *enters alone.*

KREON   My Elders, my Aunties. Our house that was once
         teeming with thieves
         Is now under our keep once again. I ask to speak
         privately with you,
         Honored counselors in domestic affairs, wise
         guardians
         Of our domestic dependent nations.
         I have ascended most humbly to this rank of power
         As trusted interpreter of days gone by—bloody bat-
         tles and tales of valor,
         Treacherous acts and land redeemed—such are my
         stories.
         The State sees me its pet, just as I would have it.
         Never would it countenance an Indian otherwise.
           Think upon our warrior-chiefs: Geronimo,

Sitting Bull, Captain Jack, Joseph.

Imprisoned and tortured they were, in those days.

I have learned from their losses

    To *smile* at my bosses

And hold an unforked tongue.

My Aunties, your Nephew asks most humbly for
    blessing

As I fill this great house with glorious treasure:
    beadwork, baskets, sealskin boats.

I speak the Great Law of Peace, Squanto's desire,
    and all the brave deeds of dying braves

Who gave up their blood for Democracy.

Recently I've made a most significant acquisition.
    The full regalia of the famed Ataoklas,

the great Crow warrior

Who rode out against the Hostiles.

I have brought it home.

Soon I will tell his story as it has never before been
    told.

Our house will be filled with glory. His name will
    be spoken with awe

And gratitude and honor. For surely he made great
    sacrifice

To kill his own for the greater Good and security of
    our homeland.

Our Tító·qan[11] will continue, and we will live in the
    land of our fathers

Because we make kinship with our countrymen, the
    Conquerors,

---

11 "Indian People"

And promise them no harm. I find myself in excel-
   lent position
To promote this message most widely. Of course,
   my Aunties, I open my hand
To my Red brothers and sisters who follow the law
   of the land.
It will go easier for them, to have a brother-
   interpreter. I can make
A great show of their returns, their ceremonies, of
   all that is human,
All that remains. But those who would be rash—
   those who hold vigil,
Who plot to take this treasure, who turn to guerilla
   means—those are the ones
I must deny.
They are not my kin who would violate the hard-
   fought laws,
And I will turn on them to preserve this house.
My Aunties, you see my heart is with my People
And my eye is on the State.

AUNTIE #3   The one who calls himself Nephew
         Speaks as Lawyer's child, as one
         Who would sign a fraudulent treaty for All.

CHORUS   The laws you call upon
      Will govern the living as the dead.

KREON   Your blessing then, my Aunties?

CHORUS   *(silence)*

KREON   Our holdings are under guard. I am secure in
        what I do.

AUNTIE #3   Many things the white man has done
            The Indian has done to his own.

KREON   Arrows from behind, I know. But do not incite a war
        against me.

> *Hesitantly, a* GUARD *approaches from behind*
> *the museum doors.*

GUARD   Sir, Director, I've come as quickly as I could
        Given the fact that I bring a message
        That I've been in no rush to deliver, knowing
        That hardly worse news could be brought
        By foot or by text or by tongue. At various times
        Both feet and tongue tried to go other ways, and
        Were it not for my honor-bound duty, not to mention
        My contractual obligation through the Interna-
            tional Organization of Museum Guards
            and Employees Union,
        I surely would not stand before you today
        Bearing the news of unbearable consequence.

KREON   And what news is that?

GUARD   First let me say in my defense:
        I know nothing of what I am about to speak.

KREON   You are a cipher.

GUARD   I did not see nor hear this thing that happened. Not
In flesh or film was it captured.

KREON   Whatever it was seems captured in your mouth.
Or in that large empty receptacle at the end of your
neck.

GUARD   It is not easy to say.

KREON   Out with it! You try my patience.

GUARD   Okay, then. Here it is:
The warrior brothers are gone.

KREON   Gone! You mean they have been moved.

GUARD   Yes. Moved. Removed. Out of the building.

KREON   What are you saying? Artifacts are missing?

GUARD   Yes.

KREON   How could this happen? Surely you are mistaken.

GUARD   I am not mistaken nor am I alone a witness of the
vault
That once was still in slumber but now speaks
The echoes of cries and footfalls, the panic of guard-
ians unaware
Of the treasure slipped through the doors. Not only
human remains are missing,

but all the magnificent testimony
of their warrior lives: warshirts and coup sticks,
beaded cuffs and painted shields.
(to CHORUS*)*
The mystery of it remains how the heist was carried
    out. The moment theft was discovered,
We locked down the grounds, hoping to
Ensnare the thief red-handed. Or thieves, shall I
say, for no one person could possibly bear
The weight of this catalogue alone.
The curious thing—we found no evidence. We found
Not a trace of entry or exit.
Not a whisper of movement
Or a shadow of sound recorded on camera.
Every eye failed us.
It was as if a wind had borne it all away, but even
    wind leaves tracks,
And we found none. A thorough search ended when
    we turned
Anxious hands upon each other. *An inside job,* we
    cried, pointing
Index fingers to each other's chests, where pounded
    hearts newly rent.
Our Union now unraveled in fears of fraternal be-
    trayal. One of us
Would succeed in deception, while all of us would
    fall. Not one of us
Can be saved, though we swear to submit to future
    inquisitions,
Give blood-oaths, and tie our souls to the poly-
    graph's quiver.

(*to* KREON)

Kind Sir, I give my word:

Each of us remained at his appointed post, yet none
of us

Bore witness to this ugly turn of events.

My heart bleeds as I speak; it is beyond explanation.

AUNTIE #3 You will find your red-handed thief.

She is red-handed indeed.

KREON   *To* CHORUS OF AUNTIES

Your words suggest that you see more than you say.

You may wish to confound me with riddles, but Elders,

Surely you see that through this theft greater things
may be stolen

Not only from me but from you. Now consider

Who wishes to strip me from this post.

Who wishes to silence my revisions, my visions, of
history

Those who see me a wolf at the door—are they the
ones you would favor?

For though I am the Headman here, I remain

A government-appointed chief, granted powers to
sign

The futures and pasts of our People.

This theft is a conspiracy

To steal from me, from you, the right to hold our
Ancestors in honor

To rule the museum, to sign the deeds, to show
what remains of our Nations

Within this nation. They will have my head, so to
  speak, when this loss comes to light.
An Indian is yet a savage, after all, under *their* law.
And truly an Indian is most capable of this sav-
  agery. My kin
Are worthy warriors, refusing captivity, serving an-
  other Order. I fear them
More than the Americans. Was it one of our own
  who did this?
I have enemies above and beside me.
    (Pause. KREON *paces, then stops.)*
But perhaps I'm taking this too personally. It could
  be no more than thieves
Who greased the hands of our guards to gain a fine
  bit of capital
For the black market, which trades in bones and
  measures in scarcity.
To them, giving life to a dead Indian is greater
Than taking life from a living one,
    although in one act
They accomplish both.

                         To GUARD

Let me tell you this: punishment awaits you
Who have been trusted with Government treasure.
  In these days
Of War and Terror it will not go lightly on you
To show the slightest crack in security. You guards
  are one tribe
Under Homeland Security, and we are here in the
  Capitol, where demands

For statesmen and tourists are most extreme. I ad-
vise you to find
The conspirators among you, to seize the hands
unfaithful
To your tribe and nation, and bring them to justice.

GUARD   May I speak a word?

KREON   Is it not obvious how much your words annoy me?

GUARD   Is it your ears or your heart that is troubled?

KREON   What do you care of my pain?

GUARD   The one who did this hurts your heart. I only hurt
your ears.

KREON   *(exasperated)* You, my man, are a pain in the ass.

GUARD   I see that, Sir. But I did not do this deed, and neither
did our men.

KREON   You did! You sold our bones and your souls.

GUARD   Ah!
This one cannot be convinced.

KREON   If you wish to convince me, bring forward the one
who did this.

KREON *retreats to his office.*

GUARD   *Calling after* KREON, *who does not hear him.*

May the perpetrator be caught! But whatever the case
I depart now for refuge with my Union, who will
defend me
Against these unwarranted claims and the defama-
tion of my men.

He leaves, heading beyond the walls of the
Museum, into the city.

The CHORUS *performs.*

AUNTIE #2   Wá·qoʔ titwatísa ná·qc.

They were living there, a handsome young man
and his sister.
One day Grizzly Bear moved into their house with
them. They lived that way
For some time, because there seemed no way to get
Grizzly Bear out.
Grizzly Bear was cruel to the sister and made her
a slave.
Grizzly Bear even made the sister use her own
hair to wipe Grizzly Bear's backside clean.
The young man was distressed and felt sorry for his
sister.
One day he was out hunting, and he accidentally
stepped on Meadowlark and broke her leg.
Auntie, he said to her, *please tell me. How can I get rid of*
Grizzly Bear?
I'll make you a madrone-stick leg if you tell me what
to do.

Meadowlark told him, *Make your house very strong so no one can get out.*

When Grizzly Bear falls asleep, sneak out quietly and set a fire around the house and burn her up.

That's the only way to get rid of her.

The young man thanked Meadowlark and made for her a new leg.

He did exactly as she told him; he set the house on fire as Grizzly Bear slept.

The young man and his sister slipped out.

Grizzly Bear woke and ran from one end to the other, trying to get out.

As everything was burning, the young man said to this sister,

Qáni,[12] *let's go now. Run and don't look back!*

He told her to come quickly, but she lagged behind.

Then *BOOM!*

There was an explosion.

The sister looked back.

Grizzly Bear called to her: *Sister-in-Law! This is yours! Take my teeth!*

The girl caught the teeth and hid them away.

Her brother asked her: *What do you hide? What did you catch?*

The girl said, *Oh nothing, nothing.*

The brother ran ahead.

He could hear her footsteps behind him.

He could hear her breath.

---

12 "Little Sister," addressive form for man

The breathing became louder.

 The footsteps became heavier.

  He continued to run.

The girl put the teeth in her mouth

 The breath was loud and heavy, very clear now

  Closer, closer, he heard her breathing

She became Grizzly Bear!

She chased her brother but he ran ahead. He took a knife

And split open the land, making a wide gulch

Difficult for Grizzly Bear to cross. He was able to cover more distance. Still,

Grizzly Bear went on tracking him.

He came to a hill and looked down. He saw some-one there.

It was Pissing Boy, jumping back and forth, singing a song.

The young man ran to Pissing Boy.

Pácqa,[13] *Little Brother, hide me! Grizzly Bear is after me!*

Pissing Boy said, *No. Not until you address me differently.*

The young man thought of every kinship term he could. *peqí·yex!*[14] and *máma!*[15]

He tried qaláca?[16] and piláqa?[17] and other kinship words.

---

13 man's younger brother addressive
14 man's brother's child/nephew addressive
15 man's sister's child/nephew addressive
16 father's father
17 mother's father

Each time, Pissing Boy said *no*. Finally he said, *ciki·wn!*[18] *Brother-in-Law!*

Hide me!

That's it! said Pissing Boy, and he hid the young man in his braids.

He went back to singing and jumping as he had done before.

Soon Grizzly Bear arrived, following the young man's tracks.

Do you see my prey around here? she asked. *I see his tracks. Where is he?*

Pissing Boy answered, *Oh, are you the only one who eats humans?*

I caught him long ago.

She laughed and said, *When did I ever eat humans?*

Pissing Boy said again: *I took him long ago.*

You're just talking nonsense, Grizzly Bear said.

I'll kill you! Pissing Boy warned.

Grizzly Bear fell on her back laughing.

And this is what Pissing Boy did. He turned and peed on his hand, then threw it in her face.

Grizzly Bear dropped dead.

That's this much of the story.

SECOND EPISODE/SCENE III

The CHORUS *notices the* GUARD *returning, bringing* ANTIKONI *with him as a prisoner.*

---

18 brother-in-law

AUNTIE #3 Who is this poor one, borne in the arms of the Guard,
Returning now? Surely she is nu·nim páplaq[19]
Antíkoni, yúʔc yiyé·ẃic[20]
Poor, unfortunate one, the child of divided blood,
divided land
Who chooses to die under one law rather than live
under two.

GUARD Here's the one you seek! Here is the one who would
steal
What by rights belongs to the State. But where is Kreon?

CHORUS *As they reply,* KREON *appears from his office.*
Koná hipá·yca.[21]

KREON ʔehé, pa·ytóqsa.[22]

GUARD My Chief, I return, once believing
That these gates would be closed to me forever,
That the only institution of the State that could ad-
mit me
Were I to admit guilt—though guiltless I would
be—is the prison,
Not your grand hall, your showcase of captivity.
Only because the Heavens favored me

---

19 "our granddaughter," maternal side
20 "poor, pitiful one"
21 "There he comes/arrives."
22 "Yes, I return/circle back."

Did I come upon this one, this girl, this thief
Carrying away the remains, bearing the treasure
  of the State
To some other resting place.
May this one soon be on her way to the Shadow-
  lands as well,
This one who loves the dead
And may my honor be restored by her passing.

KREON   And this one, how did you catch her? Was she yet on
     the grounds?

GUARD   She was bearing the bones away herself. Just beyond
     the gate.

KREON   My man, you know the nature of this charge? You
     testify to truth
     in matters of a federal crime?

GUARD   My sight is true, and my words follow.
     The appearance of this girl with dry blood, now
      dust on her hands
     And ancient words on her tongue
     Turns me from traitor to hero, from man to myth.
      Here is your body of evidence!
     Her body has much more in common with yours,
      my Chief,
     As I share not blood nor favor
     With this Indian girl.
     Forgive me, Sir, for speaking so forthrightly.

I fear for you now under the law
As the Feds will see you as accomplice, and me
As the noble whistleblower, and I
Will be afforded every protection
that would be yours by rank,
  but trumped by blood.

KREON   *To* ANTIKONI

ʔikú·ytimx![23]
Speak to me in the language of truth.

ANTIKONI hi'ná·kata.[24]

KREON   *To* GUARD

You heard her.

                    Pause. KREON *stares at* GUARD, *who doesn't*
                                        know what to do.

GUARD Sir, with all respect. I don't speak—

KREON Ah! If only you didn't speak at all! How quickly pos-
          session changes your register.
          You who earlier cowered in fear

---

23 "Tell the truth!" Literally: (speak) truth-language!
24 "She carried (something) out." The root of the verb is "out," and the
prefix is "carry," placing emphasis on the action of going out. Here Antíkoni
uses an older convention of Nez Perce speech, employing third-person form
to express intensity.

Now speak as a master. But you have not mastered
our language, have you?
Perhaps you thought it dead?

GUARD No. No, Sir. Not dead at all.

KREON Very well, then. Perhaps you are not entirely worth-
less, although your greatest
Capital is your captive.
Do you not wish to know how she has assessed
herself?

GUARD *nods anxiously.*

KREON She said she is guilty.

ANTIKONI Uncle, I object to your translation. Guilt is not on my
tongue or my heart.
Truly I am most free of guilt.
I said only that I carried out.

KREON You carried out a crime.

ANTIKONI Again you translate me wrongly. You move me across,
From the arms of my family to the chains of the
State.
You twist my tongue to unlock your laws.
I do pity you, Uncle, for you have long ago admitted
yourself
To this prison, a darkness of another name.

KREON   And do you say, My Child, that there is no difference
          In the prison between the inmate and the warden,
          Though both abide within? Surely you know better.

                         Gestures for the GUARD *to leave. He departs.*

ANTIKONI Are not the prisoner and the warden equally made of
             flesh? Are they not equally
          Bound to the laws of Creation, to the turn of the
             Earth? Living and dead,
          Humans belong to the same Order that turns and
             turns around itself,
          Not to these unholy states
              of suspension: the prisoner doing time, the arti-
              fact preserved.
          These are human laws—though they are not
             humane—that would defy
          Ancient laws. These unjust laws make a captive of
          Time itself.

KREON   Your weakness, Little One, is that you cannot calcu-
             late difference
              in degree or kind.
          It makes for rather brittle politics.
          Perhaps I may interest you in a story.
          I have recently acquired a rare collection of
              projectile points
          Made by the famous Yahi Indian, Ishi.
          When he lived—or as you may say, when he was a
              captive—at the museum in California

he occupied himself by knapping arrowheads
from the glass bottoms of bottles.
Spectators came from far and wide to admire him
as he worked. His creations
are most beautiful: impossibly long, elegant,
and perfectly formed.
But completely nonfunctional. Shoot one of those at
a mountain lion and the point would snap in two.

ANTIKONI How dare you translate Ishi this way? You cast him as
an artist in his studio,
not the living exhibit he truly was—
Though I hardly call it *living*, a human being alone.
It's not how we were meant to live.
The museum preserves the life of things longing to
die, while
Killing the Man, the last of his kind, whose tongue
cruelly died before him.
Ishi's admirers loved him to death.

KREON I do not dispute that he was a captive. I dispute that
he was a slave.
Though no one remained with whom he could
speak, his language remains.
Our languages do not die, though sometimes they
sleep.
Ishi sang to himself, he recorded his voice, and he
laughed in the faces of those curious fools.
But Child, you're missing the *point*, shall we say, of
my story.
Shall I spell it out? Your politics are glass arrowheads.

Perfect, beautiful, and brittle.

And, need we say? Absurdly outmoded for the time.

ANTIKONI   What you call politics I call waq̓íʼswit—a way of life.

KREON   It is a way of death. Their law makes it so.

Your deeds, however holy to you, will not go
unpunished.

ANTIKONI   Oh, to confound justice with laws!

You abide by the State, by laws made by man and
upheld by force.

You abide with the State, you lie with your colonizers.

Surely you know as I do a greater Law, our
tamá·lwit[25]

That our Elder Brother set the Earth in motion,

And the Earth lies with its head to the East,

Its feet to the West, and its arms to the North and
the South.

When we die we likewise lie down in the same way

The head to the East, the feet to the West

We must care for the body this way

This is the way to care for the body from the begin-
ning of time

From time immemorial, for eternal time.

KREON   And was this Law on the heart of brave Ataoklas,

A Cavalry scout, who paused not a moment before
taking the blood

---

25 Law

Of his own flesh, Polynaikas? Did he make a proper
  grave
For his own brother, the son of his own mother? Or
  was he
Just a treasonous dog?
I dare say you have more kinship with me than with
  that one—
Though you, like Ataoklas, may bring down your
  sibling with you.
    Consider this:
It is I who redeem those brothers, not you.
I bring their story to life, I redeem what remains—
What remains of being human.
Love, betrayal, tragedy: by these grand themes
I return to the departed their flesh, their humanity.
It is the story, not the body, that matters, that endures.
The physical body, the blood, is dust. But the story
  walks and breathes.
I have given my life to that.
I have chosen the living over the dead.

ANTIKONI   You've chosen to *make a living* over our dead.

KREON   So judgmental! And tell me, would you prefer that I
  endure
Removal
    from my office? Or perhaps that I face
Relocation
    to another post. But knowing you, I imagine
    only

Termination
> will satisfy you.

Don't be a fool, My Child. If I give up this post, it
> will hardly cease to exist.

No! It will be filled by the So·yá·po·[26] and his lies. I
> won't have it.

Through diligence and obsequious posture I've gained
A most coveted post, and happily feigned
Pacification. It's the only path to power.

It's a shame that every war comes down to this:
> A battle between the Hostiles and the Friendlies.

I regret that you've chosen the other side, as I will
> have no choice

But to prove through punishment of you—and your
> sister for good measure—

That I'm a good soldier for the State. It's a sacrifice
> for the greater Good, you see.

Surely I'm speaking your language now.

> > *(Calls offstage to* GUARD*)*

GUARD! Remove this criminal from my sight.
> Lock her up

And her sister beside her.

> > GUARD *comes and escorts* ANTIKONI *off*
> > *stage.* KREON *paces, visibly distressed.*

AUNTIE #3   There's a story I know.
> Not so long ago, there was a woman

---

26 "White Man"

And she had powerful medicine. She was the best gambler

Of anyone around. No one could beat her at Stick Game

Though many, many tried. Her power was known all around

And when she died

One of her rivals, a man from her mother's band

Took two finger bones from her hand

And made a pair of gambling sticks.

This man became the most powerful then, virtually unbeatable.

People came from all around to lose to him.

His luck was fantastic.

He had those gambling bones, you see.

But at night

The ghost of the dead woman would appear
    And insist that the man sleep with her.

Night after night, she bothered him. She seduced him.

She would not let him rest.

Finally he gave up. He returned the bones

And the ghost went away.

This is a true story.

THIRD EPISODE/SCENE IV

HAIMON *joins* KREON *on stage.*

KREON   My Son, two paths were laid open before you, but I have chosen

To close one road for your own good. And for the
good of nú·nim Tító·qan.[27]
Is your heart reconciled to this upward path—do
you follow me?
Or do you prefer to pursue your bride on another
journey, surely doomed?

HAIMON Tó·ta[28], I am your true son, and true to you. Even as
you have power to
Condemn the one who has crossed you, the State
may do the same
Ten times over to you. Your punishment of her is
mere discipline,
But if the State comes for you, you will pay in blood.
Not only you, but all Tító·qan will suffer, if you are
Removed.

KREON Surely, you are keen to history. The State makes
grand monuments
To Indian defeat. Metacomet was drawn and quar-
tered. The bodyless head of
Captain Jack was sent on a transcontinental tour.
Geronimo was paraded in chains.
And Leonard Peltier—ah, just to say the name
Is to utter our state of helplessness. Helpless but not
hopeless we remain
Within the walls of this foreign nation. We are oc-
cupied by them

27 "our Indian people"
28 "Father" addressive

And preoccupied by our desire
To bend their laws, not break them.
I am now Director of this Museum, this Palace of
    treasure,
And I am Master of all the State surveys.
You, too, my Son, may walk this path that I now
    forge for you
And those who come after. You may earn your law
    degree
And then you may decree
The futures of the living and the dead. Let fair
    Antíkoni cry out
In defense of a cosmic Order that binds us
Blood and bone to land, that the dead may be
    mourned
In a proper way, in their proper place, and that the
    living may then live.
I have no use for Eternal Laws! That indeed is the
    point.
I put my effort into what I may affect. Or rather:
    infect.
Under federal law the only constant is change. So
    we must constantly
Change, shift our shapes, perform for them what
    they wish to see
Then we shall have our Way, by minding their
    watch.
This is how we've survived, and how we've
    undermined
The United States of Surveillance.

CHORUS   *(singing)* Oh, say can you see!

HAIMON   Tó·ta, your acquaintance with the stories told from
          long ago
          And the battles won by canny maneuvers
          Show that you are wise indeed to the ways of the
          world.
          You are right to keep your eye on the State
          But might I mention, with all humility, that perhaps
          you turn an ear
          To the cries of nú·nim Titó·qan. There's quite a bit
          of talk, you see
          And it is only in defense of you that I dare mention it.
          Indian Country is aflame with rumors, and there
          may be trouble for you
          If you don't show leniency to the One Who Car-
          ried Out,
          For she is most venerated and honored among them
          As brave and upright. If you punish her harshly you
          may be rewarded
          But a bounty will only tip the scales in her favor.
          Indeed, she has such sympathy among our kin
          Punishment will only breed more dissent. And *they*
          will call for your head.
          They are not so helpless as you may think.

CHORUS   Surely the son speaks the truth.

KREON   *(to* CHORUS*)*
          This one is yet a youth, caught up in the romance

Of a youthful act. Politics become more subtle with age,
When one is less inclined to move so quickly.
(*to* HAIMON)
Is your heart yet with this girl who defies me?

HAIMON Tóta, my heart as yours is with our People
And from their hearts they defend her hand.

KREON Would you have a woman setting the rules?
If you don't respect me, Son, at least you should re-
spect the office.

HAIMON Yes, Father, the office was made for the White Man,
For his desires and powers alone. And yet
You have taken his place. I remind you only that
you remain
An Indian. And an Indian is no one without his
Tribe.

KREON More romantic words from you! The Tribe, the
Tribe!
That I could be rescued from the Tribe!
I have no use for tribal politics.
Let me be my own man.
No one pulling my strings, not the Tribe or the State
Or the sentimental appeals of my faithless son.

HAIMON Ɂikúˑyn, Tóta, I speak the language of justice, not
sentiment.
If you destroy her, others will fall, too.

KREON Who is in place to defend our dead? I alone
Have the power to protect them, and all our patri-
mony here.
I will not be dispossessed. I am on my heart.

HAIMON I see the truth of this. ʔi·nim čaʔá timine.[29]

HAIMON *leaves.*

KREON Let him try to save her.
(to CHORUS*)*
Aunties, what is your counsel?

AUNTIE #4 Wá·qoʔ titwatísa ná·qc.
They were living there; many people were camped
together. And every morning
The hunters would go out. When they brought
home meat, they would
Distribute it to everyone. This way, no one was hungry.
There were five brothers, and the oldest one was
married.
The five brothers went hunting one day.
The oldest one shot a deer, and as he was butcher-
ing it in the mountains
He cut his hand. He brought his hand to his mouth
and sucked the blood
From his wound, and as he did this, he realized that
the taste of his own blood

---

29 Literally: "I am exactly on my heart"; figuratively: "I am on target."

Was *delicious*. He began to crave the taste of blood, and
Without being able to control himself, he began to
 eat this own arm.
He found that he could not stop. Soon he consumed
 his entire arm,
Then his other arm, his body, and his two legs.
He did not come home for several days, and soon
 his brothers
Went to look for him. The man became hideous; he
 was only bones and sinew,
   and he carried his intestines in one hand like a
   rope.
When he saw his younger brother coming, he hid in
 the bushes and called out his brother's name. The
 brother came, and when he was close
The man who was now a cannibal jumped out and
 lassoed him with his intestine-rope.
   He tied up his brother and ate him.
Each day another brother came searching, and the
 Cannibal caught each one.
   He killed and ate his own brothers.
In the meantime, the wife and their little baby were
 living
Beside the river with the people. When her husband
 and then his brothers
Did not come home, the people became worried.
We're going to move camp, they said to the woman, *and
 you should come with us.*
No, she said. *I will wait here for my husband and his broth-
 ers to return,*

And we will join you later.

The people did not want to leave her, but she insisted.

She stayed there in her tipi, encamped by the river.

One day she heard a strange sound:

    Clackity-clack, clackity-clack, and then her hus-
band's voice.

He was coming down the hill, his bones clacking
hard upon each other, and

Calling her name. He carried his intestines in both
hands.

    Clackity-clack he came.

Truly! She saw that he was hideous. She picked up
the baby

    but soon her husband was there at the tipi door.

Oh, my child, he cooed. *Let me hold him.*

The woman could see how he was eyeing the tender
flesh of the baby.

Of course, the woman said. *Just let me wash him for you
first.*

You wait here while I go to the river and prepare him for you.

The Cannibal sat down to wait, and the wife slipped
out of the tipi with the baby. As she left, she
grabbed a wooden spoon and hid it under her arm.

She ran with the baby to the river's edge.

Willows! she called out to the trees. *When he looks for
us, you sing so that he thinks we are yet here.*

Shoo-shoo, the willow trees sang.

The woman threw the wooden spoon to the ground.

Become a canoe! she cried. And the spoon became a
canoe, and she

Placed it in the river with her child, and it carried
  them to the village ahead
Where her people were encamped.
She arrived there and told the people about her
  cannibal husband,
And thus they knew what had become of him and
  his brothers.
In the meantime, the Cannibal became suspicious.
  He went down to the river
Where the willows were singing, *shoo-shoo-shoo.*
He was angry at this deception and beat the willows
  horribly.
Downriver, the people moved camp again, and the
  Cannibal never found them.
That's all.

FOURTH EPISODE/SCENE V

The blind medicine singer TAIRASIAS *is led on
stage by a boy. He calls out to the* CHORUS.

TAIRASIAS Aunties! I come to report what I have seen
That you may discern if it is past, or present, or future
I have seen Antíkoni, and she lives yet among the
  dead.

KREON *enters from his office.*

KREON Grandfather, what message do you bring?

TAIRASIAS I declare again a truth you've heard many times.

I repeat the Ancient Laws, and the longing of the
living
To properly abide with the Dead. Your power de-
pends on this.

KREON   If I am toppled I will not be easily replaced.

TAIRASIAS   Care not for your own head but consider the barren
skulls
Of those who came before. They like you dwelt in
flesh and love
And now desire to rest. As long as human remains
are held
As trophies in this endless war, the humans remain
Less than fully alive. So grant them their lives by
honoring their dead.

KREON   It is not so simple as that. I cannot release that which
belongs to the State.

TAIRASIAS   Grandson, when you hold captive the Dead, you en-
slave the living.
The talons of the State wrap 'round the bones of the
departed
And dig deep into the flesh of those who remain.
You yet may change your course. For what can be
gained
By killing again those who are already dead?
Perhaps
Your ambition has made you blind, more blind
than I, who see

That the museum is a Cannibal: consuming the liv-
ing, piling up the dead.

Grandson, I worry for you.

But perhaps you cannot help yourself.

Perhaps you've tasted your own blood, and found
it pleasing.

I'm warning you! Do not feed on yourself.

KREON   Grandfather, your words are sharp arrows

That you should aim at another target. I am not the
enemy here.

If you persist in drawing these disturbing visions I
may have no choice

But to be in the market for a new Medicine Man.
I happen to know

Some reasonably priced Shamans who charge by
the hour.

TAIRASIAS   By all means! I offer my words most freely, and prom-
ise great returns.

But if you prefer praise, and blind adoration of your
rule,

You will certainly get what you pay for.

You see that this is a world of exchanges
And words will not redeem the dead.

The State demands this: blood for bone.

It has never been any other way.

KREON   I offer my mind, not my head. My words, not my
mouth.

TAIRASIAS   Ah, you see: the Ancient One was delivered through
the mouths of our kin.

Though not, as you say, by words,
>nor by law,
>nor by cries for justice.

Only a swab would redeem him. The State demands DNA.

Openmouthed and brokenhearted, they offered
their bodies up
>to finally bring the Ancient One home.
>That is blood for bone.

You give up your sister's child. You offer
>blood for bone, blood for bone.

KREON   Grandfather, that was another time.

TAIRASIAS   Perhaps another time, not a different time.

In the time before the humans came, Coyote set
many laws in motion.

He separated the Sun and Moon, so they would not
be cannibals;

He flattened Rattlesnake's head and smashed Grizzly Bear's nose;

He pried open the wings of Butterfly, and stripped
Muskrat's tail.

He gave the Gophers eyes to see. He did many,
many things
>To make this world ready for humans.
>*The humans are coming soon.*

Grandson, look around. And you will see.

KREON   Old Man, you are as maddening as those Aunties.

What kind of Advisor

Cannot answer a question straight?

TAIRASIAS   *(pause)*

Here is your straight answer then:

What kind of human makes captive his kin?

He gestures, and the BOY *leads him away.*

AUNTIE #5   Wá·qoʔ titwatísa ná·qc.

After Pissing Boy killed Grizzly Bear, he went to visit his five sisters.

To the first one he said, *Né·neʔ, give me some bone marrow.*

But she enjoyed the bones herself. He asked the same of each sister,

And each one refused him, until he came to *lay-míwt,*[30] the youngest one.

When did they ever give you anything? she asked.
Here, take this one, it's yours, break it.

So he broke the bone and took the marrow, and every so often

He would hand it back, to feed the handsome man he had hid in his braids.

When it was time for bed, Pissing Boy asked the oldest sister:

Né·neʔ, can I sleep in your bed?

---

30 In Nez Perce stories that have this feature, the littlest/youngest one (*laymíwt*) solves the problem.

Hamó·lic,[31] *no, you wet the bed too much!*

Again he asked each of his sisters, and every one said no

Except for *laymíwt*, the youngest one, who said:

When have they ever given you a place to sleep? Come, I will show you where we can sleep.

And there they went to sleep. Pissing Boy brought out the handsome man

And told his sister: *Here, I brought this man for you.*

In the morning the other sisters saw the man and they were jealous.

They wanted him too! But Pissing Boy said:

You did not give me anything,

You must leave your brother-in-law alone.

The young man lived there with them from that time, and would go hunting.

Pissing Boy told him: *When you hunt, don't go over the ridge.*

Don't follow anything over the ridge, do not chase it there.

One day the young man shot a deer, but it ran from him, wounded.

The young man ran to the top of ridge and looked over.

For a long time he stayed there.

He saw the buck lying dead at the roots of a big pine tree.

He thought: *I wonder why my brother-in-law said not to go over this ridge.*

---

31 Term of endearment: "adorable one," "cutie-pie"

I don't see anything amiss. I'm going to go!

He ran to the deer and began to dress it out, but very soon it grew dark.

All at once he became surrounded by big-bellied people.

Oh, so this is the reason he told me not to go over the ridge!

The people tore into the deer, and the young man escaped up a tree.

Soon the big-bellied people found him. All night long they tried to get him down,

but the young man stayed in the tree.

In the morning it became light, and the big-bellied people could no longer see.

It's dark now, they said. *Let's sleep now, since it is our bedtime.*

They slept in a circle around him.

In the meantime, Pissing Boy became worried about his brother-in-law.

He must have gone over the ridge!

Pissing Boy made himself ready, then he went to find his brother-in-law.

He came to the tree where the big-bellied people were sleeping.

Now you come down, he called to the man, *And I will carry you out.*

Pissing Boy ran around the circle and exploded their bellies with his foot.

He said, *These people are Cannibals from long ago. They would eat everyone, everything around. But now*

I have exploded them with my foot.

Pissing Boy threw their bodies into the sky, saying:

You will remain

high in the sky,

and never again will you do anything to anyone.

He scattered them like that, and said:

Now everyone will say,

"They are just stars who disappear in the day, and ap-

pear in the dark."

After that, Pissing Boy took his brother-in-law home. He had defeated

the big-bellied people, and after that they lived in peace.

That's all.

DRUM   *(The* DRUM *beats.*[32]*)*

KREON *paces, agitated. Shortly, a* MESSENGER
arrives, interrupting the drumming.

MESSENGER   Wise Counselors, I bring the news that no Seer could have seen

The House of Kreon is most surely disturbed

Discontent rages from without and within. It cannot stand.

Yet neither will it fall. Instead it remains *in media res*

---

32 The rhythm for the Drum is common for hand drum: *de-dum, de-dum, de-dum* (as a heartbeat).

So like a diorama: life suspended and death made
    animate.
With the help of Haimon, the Captive is released
Her whereabouts and fate unknown. She has re-
    moved herself
Beyond the reach of human touch.

> *The image of* ANTIKONI *appears on a large*
> *screen, center stage.* MESSENGER *departs.*

CHORUS   Oh, Antíkoni, Poor Little One,
    We see you in your tomb, suspended
    Between the living and the dead.

ANTIKONI   And here I shall remain, along with the dead
    My life as theirs suspended, just as that of my kin
    Who find no comfort in grief, whose grief can never
        begin
    And thus will never end.
    In this world in-between, my voice and visage live on
    To those not-yet-human what human laws may do
        to interrupt time, to stop the Earth
    From turning and turning around itself, how such
        laws disturb
    The Order of the world. For this cause I sacrifice
    The warmth of flesh on mine, the company of hu-
        man voice
    My sister's laugh, my lover's touch
    I retreat to this living tomb, this landless home, to
    This place that is both nowhere and everywhere at
        once.

> ANTIKONI's *image on the screen multiplies to*
> *a 3 x 3 grid of images.*

Here I will not age, nor bear
Children for the next generation. I shall live
Though it cannot be called *living*, a human being alone.

> *The screen image, still a grid, is replaced by*
> *line-drawn avatars.*

> HAIMON *and* ISMENE *enter. They try to touch*
> ANTIKONI's *image. The image continues*
> *to multiply to a 4 x 4 grid, then a 5 x 5 grid.*
> *When* ISMENE *or* HAIMON *touches an avatar,*
> *the image returns to* ANTIKONI's *face.*

ISMENE Né·ne', return to the world of the living. Listen:
You take my life with you. You have my heart.

HAIMON Sí·kstiwa·,[33] surely our Eternal Laws withstand the
current Order.
I beg you to return from this No Man's Land, your
refuge in this war
For your retreat exposes us as it hides you—we are
bound with you.

> KREON *enters the stage and the* CHORUS *begins to drum.*
> KREON, ISMENE, *and* HAIMON *turn their backs to the*
> *audience and address* ANTIKONI's *screen images.*

---

33 "Darling" or "dearest"; best friend, partner; literally: "nestmate"

Lights dim on the main stage, so that the light
from the screens is dominant.

As the lights dim, additional DRUMMERS
take their place in a circle around the audience.

(As each one speaks, their voices overlap. They
chant each phrase several times, with differing
inflections, to create a cacophonous sound. As
they speak, encircling DRUMMERS *begin to*
DRUM, *amplifying the sound.)*

ANTIKONI   Oh, to confound Justice with Laws!
What is denied the Dead is denied the living ten
times again.
We remain captives with them.

ISMENE   Elder Brother set the Earth in motion, turning it
to the right
We must care for the body this way
From time immemorial, for eternal time.

HAIMON   You remain an Indian.
And an Indian is no one without his Tribe.

KREON   This is how we've survived,
and how we've undermined
The United States of Surveillance.

CHORUS   The humans are coming soon
Already they are coming this way.

ANTIKONI, ISMENE, HAIMON,
KREON, *and* CHORUS *stop at the moment*
ANTIKONI*'s face again fills the screen.*
DRUMS *continue. On screen,* ANTIKONI
lights a sage bundle and the smoke curls
upward. She looks out at the audience.

The DRUM *beats a hard beat.*

Lights out. Screen with ANTIKONI*'s face*
remains a second longer, then blacks out, with
the final beat of the DRUM.

Acknowledgments

This book was a long time in the making, and I have many people to thank.

For their generosity and patience as teachers of Nez Perce language, I am grateful to Haruo Aoki, Phillip Cash Cash, Angel Sobotta, Milton Davis Jr., Bessie Scott, Florene Davis, Albert Redstar Andrews, Harold Crook, and the community of Nez Perce speakers. Special thanks to my late auntie, Theresa Eagle, for giving me my first words.

I have been fortunate to know many writers who are mentors and friends, and I have benefitted from their generosity as readers. For a multitude of gifts I thank Kathleen Holt, Renae Watchman, Alan Mikhail, Phil Cash Cash, Lisa Brooks, Luis Alberto Urrea, Ralph Rodriguez, Craig Santos Perez, John Higgins, Shelley Fisher Fishkin, Bryan Wolf, Richard White, Lois Deckert, Mark Trahant, Fae Ng, and Sherman Alexie. Many cherished colleagues read, shaped, and supported my work. For equal parts friendship and brilliance I am grateful to Jen Rose Smith, Meredith Palmer, Tom Biolsi, Mattie Harper, Christian Paiz, Philip Deloria, Jake Kosek, Leigh Raiford, Jennifer DeVere Brody, Khalil Johnson, Meg Noodin, Shari Huhndorf, Paige Raibmon, John Borrows, Bayley Marquez, Juliet Kunkel, Ramya Janandharan, Tala Khanmalek, Shokoofeh Rajabzadeh, David

Henkin, Andy Shanken, Phenocia Bauerle, Wanda Alarcon, Funie Hsu, Erica Boas, Hertha Sweet Wong, Kathleen Donegan, Leti Volpp, Sabine Meyer, Alan Palaez Lopez, Gerard Ramm, Rachel Lim, Carmen Foghorn, Blake Hausman, Margaret Rhee, Janey Lew, Yomaira Figueroa, Andrew Garrett, Julia Nee, Linda Rugg, Kathleen McCarthy, Susan Schweik, Reid Gomez, Marianne Constable, Line Mikkelsen, Cathy Choy, Mark Rifkin, Nirvana Tanoukhi, Lisa Tatonetti, Andrew Ramer, Brenda Child, Jeani O'Brien, Esther Ramer, Brian DeLay, David Palumbo-Liu, and Dylan Robinson.

For assistance in bringing the work to light, I am grateful for the kind gestures of David Treuer, Joy Harjo, Alan Mikhail, Craig Santos Perez, David Chariandy, Ralph Rodriguez, Julia Masnik, Jill Stauffer, Robert Warrior, Kirby Brown, Ernest Stromberg, Margaret Jacobs, and Rich Wandschneider. Enormous thanks to Jack Shoemaker and everyone and Counterpoint Press and Catapult and the artist Marcus Amerman for making this a beautiful book.

In autumn 2016 I was fortunate to hold a visiting fellowship at the Bard Graduate Center in New York and during that time wrote much of *Antíkoni*. Many thanks to Peter N. Miller, Aaron Glass, and everyone at the BGC for providing a beautiful, stimulating, and supportive place to work. The first performance of *Antíkoni* was a staged reading held at the Phoebe A. Hearst Museum of Anthropology at UC Berkeley in November 2018. This experiment in singing to the ancestors was made possible by the generous support of Shannon Jackson and Art + Design; Benjamin Porter and the staff at the Hearst Museum; Lisa Wymore and Theatre, Dance, and Performance Studies; Mark Griffith and the Department of Classics; Marianne Constable and the Department of Rhetoric; Andrew Garrett and the Department

of Linguistics; and the gifted crew of directors, actors, artists, and musicians who brought the play to life: Michael St. Clair, Jennif(f)er Tamayo, Kimberly Skye Richards, Christian Nagler, Keevin Hesuse, Carolyn Smith, Rose Escalano, Fantasia Painter, Skye Chayame Fierro, Ines Hernandez-Avila, Phillip Cash Cash, Benjamin Arsenault, Angel Sobotta, Anna Marie Sharpe, Joel Sedano, Thomas Tallerico, Kara Poon, Chia Yu Shih, Illan Halpern, and Sarah Biscarra Dilley.

Recently I came across a Nez Perce word, ʔatakaʔámyac, which when used as an adjective means "prosperous, affluent, well-provided," and as a noun means "a child with many relatives." This word surely describes the wealth for which I am most grateful. Unending thanks to my relations: Mom and Dad, my brothers, Daniel and John, and their families; my children, Twyla and Diego; my uncles, aunts, and many cousins, especially Kathy, Mary Ann, Jerry, Kevin, Woodrow, Rose, Vickey, and their families; my dearest friends, Kathleen and Alex, Kathy and Josh, Sheri and Jerome, Imtiaz, Stephanie, Sharee, Tia and Luke, Justus and Vanessa, Irwin and Joan, Ralph, Khalil, Nathan, Haruo, Phil, and Renae.

Much love and gratitude to all the beadworkers, whose work endures from the past and carries us into the future.

Notes

Written source materials for Nez Perce language and stories include Haruo Aoki, *Nez Perce Dictionary* (University of California Press, 1994); Haruo Aoki and Deward E. Walker Jr., *Nez Perce Oral Narratives* (University of California Press, 1989); Archie Phinney, *Nez Perce Texts* (Columbia University Press, 1934). Translations and errors are my own.

The newspaper article quoted in "The News of the Day" is from "A Fight with the Hostiles," *The New York Times*, December 30, 1890, 1.

The Dick Gregory album referenced in "Fish Wars" is *The Two Sides of Dick Gregory* (1963).

The Grizzly Bear story in "Falling Crows" is found in *Native American Arts of the Columbia Plateau: The Doris Swayze Bounds Collection of Native American Artifacts*, ed. Susan E. Harless (High Desert Museum/University of Washington Press, 1998).

For *Antigone* by Sophocles, I consulted the translation and commentary by Reginald Gibbons and Charles Segal (Oxford University Press, 2003).

BETH PIATOTE is an associate professor of Native American studies at the University of California, Berkeley. She holds a PhD from Stanford University, is the author of numerous scholarly essays and creative works, and is the recipient of multiple awards and fellowships. She is Nez Perce enrolled with Colville Confederated Tribes and lives in the San Francisco Bay Area with her two children.